A Bite Full Of Death

A Monster Romance

S.J. Stewart

S.J. Stewart

A NOTE TO MY FAMILY

LISTEN.
We're all adults here. I'm going to do this thing where I warn you this is a racey book, the kind that used to have naked people on the cover, abs bared and the whole shebang. You're going to tell me you're proud of me and my writing so of course, you're going to read this book.
COOL.
Cool, cool, cool, cool.
Read it. Enjoy it. Buy it and put it on the shelf and never read past this page. Do whatever makes you happy, but remember who I am as a person. Don't bring it up unless you fully intend for me to talk about it ... because I will.
YOU KNOW I WILL!
EVERY STEAMY DETAIL!
You've been warned.

CAUTION

BEFORE YOU READ

This book may have some themes that may be unsuitable for some readers. We have all walked very different paths and had to overcome obstacles that may have left us scarred. Though these scars make us unique, sometimes there are things in this world that can make those scars feel like fresh wounds. Because of this, we have to take precautions.

Within these pages, there will be scenes of violence that may include some blood and gore, death, and murder. There are scenes with cannibalism, grave digging and grave robbing. There are scenes with explicit sexual content that may not be suitable for younger readers. This is a dark romance with some romantic situations that reflect the character's sadism and may be trigger for some readers.

Though it is not my intention to willfully omit any triggers, I may have missed some situations that may require one. If that is the case, please feel free to reach out to me through my website or through my social media and I will happily add it to the triggers page. These links/addresses are listed at the back of the book.

Reader's discretion is advised.

To all those whose bite is worse than their bark.

A BITE FULL OF DEATH

A

FULL OF

SJ STEWART

1

POE

THE DOOR TO HER house slammed off the wall in the entryway with enough force to knock down a photo. She ignored the sound of the glass shattering as her hands ripped at the delicate fabric of the man's shirt. Buttons joined the shattered glass on the floor as she ran her hands over the expanse of his toned chest. Taut skin pulled over muscle she knew he likely worked endlessly for. Her eyes roamed over his olive skin, darkened by the sun, until she reached behind him and slammed the door shut.

A chuckle left him as she pulled off a heel and chucked it over her shoulder. Her other shoe followed as she reached her hand behind her and unzipped her dress. She shoved it off her shoulders, letting the black, slinky fabric pool around her feet before she strut bare toward him.

She hadn't bothered with panties tonight, she knew she'd have no use for them.

Hungry eyes roamed over her bare body. "Eager, are we?" He had the kind of voice she knew made people cream their panties. It was deep, a bellow that hit their core. Primal and sexy. She couldn't deny she liked it as he undid his belt.

Poe's eyes were on his hands. They were strong. Veins made endless paths under his skin and she hoped the flesh of his palms would be rough. That they'd move across her skin with blissful resistance, the way only hands weathered by hard work could. Reaching into his pants, he pulled the length of him out.

It was — unimpressive.

Not short, but not overly long. Thick enough to get the job done, but dwarfed in his big hands. No matter, Poe wasn't picky. A dick was a dick if it got the job done, and she would make sure it did.

"You like what you see, baby?" he asked, confidence dripped from every word.

Not particularly. No, she'd better not be honest. Men could be such babies when their cocks were involved. Better to play the part she knew he wanted. "Mhmm," she moaned low in her throat.

"Then come over here and get it."

Poe leapt into his arms. She wrapped her legs tightly around his waist, using her hold on his neck to lift her just enough to position the head of him at her entrance.

Fuck, she needed this.

Her stomach rumbled with a hunger no food could sate and she felt the way her mind wandered back to thoughts dripped in sexual positions and cum. She just needed a good ride to get her mind out of the proverbial gutter.

She didn't wait, didn't want to hear what he would say next. Instead, she lowered her weight and let him fill her — as much as he could. Poe arched her back as she lifted herself and rolled her hips. She needed her clit to rub against him, needed the extra stimulation to get this done as he wrapped his hand under her thighs and turned so her back hit her front door.

The slam of her weight against the stained glass knocked the wind out of her, but she didn't need to breathe. Breathing right now wouldn't add anything. If she were honest, the loss of breath only helped her along, much like the tight grip of his hand on her throat would have. The threat of him squeezing the life from her with each thrust, taking her a step closer to Death, made her gaze into the beautiful face of her deliverer as she stood at the precipice of her pleasure was a turn on all its own.

Danger only made it that much better. Pain was the icing on top of a dessert she knew she shouldn't indulge in, but she couldn't help herself. She needed it like most people needed to breathe.

He used his hold on her thighs to slam her down onto his balls. Filling her up as much as he could with each thrust. The sound of their flesh slapping together was music to her ears as she shoved two of her fingers in his mouth.

His brows dropped in confusion, but he ran his tongue over her fingers just like she knew he would.

"Good boy," she praised as she removed her fingers and reached behind her. She arched her back even more before she sunk the length of her fingers into her wet pussy right alongside his cock.

"Fuck," he breathed.

Poe tightened her walls around them both as he continued his brutal pace.

It wasn't enough. It never would be. Not for her.

Saliva pooled in her mouth as muscles moved over his jaw with each thrust. His nostrils flared as he swallowed back his moans like a selfish thing, refusing to gift her with the sound of his praise. The guttural noise of satisfaction she knew wanted to break free from his chest.

She moved her hand, keeping pace with him, and his eyes snapped open as he looked at her.

"Are you close?" he asked with each breath.

Not even close. "Yes," she lied. She would get there.

"Good," he huffed. "I'm going to come."

Her eyes went past him to the Grandfather clock at the bottom of the stairs. It had barely been five minutes. Such was the norm for a lot of mortal men, she realized. Especially the ones she sought out.

"Mhmm," she nodded and let her face fall into the space between his shoulder and neck. She moved her hand, keeping pace, ready to milk him for all he was worth. Though that wasn't the prize, not here.

A groan escaped him as his thrusts became erratic.

Poe opened her mouth and dragged her tongue against the flesh of his neck. It made him quicken his pace.

She waited for the perfect moment, for her to feel the desperation in each pull of his hands on her thighs before she sunk her teeth into him.

Her whole body tightened like a coil and then released. Her thighs shook as the sweet taste of him filled her mouth. Her stomach tensed as it was finally satisfied, her inner walls tightened, holding him captive as she rode him through her orgasm. The slow roll of her hips made her clit rub against him, and she clamped her jaw tighter on his shoulder. Her eyes rolled back in rapture.

Fuck, that's good.

He exploded. A feral groan left him as his thrusts slowed and she felt the gentle throb of him. The heat of his cum poured into her, icing her fingers. She pulled her hand free, letting her feet drop to the floor as he softened inside her and then left her completely. The heat of him left slow trails down her inner thighs as she kept her hands wrapped around his neck, on her toes to bridge the gap in their heights.

Her fangs leaving his neck were silent, but she slurped the last taste of him into her mouth before she sighed.

The relief that filled her was immeasurable. She imagined it was much like the first meal after someone was sure they would die of starvation. A satisfaction made all the sweeter by the thought it would never come — or it would come too late.

She opened her eyes and looked up into his.

They were glassy. Dull. Lifeless.

A smile was frozen on his face, even though his lips had already started to lose their pinkish hue.

Poe cupped his chin in her hands and took one last look at his face. The face of someone she knew was a bad person. Who had intimidated people at the bar, barked at the bartender as though she was beneath him, and flashed the gun in his belt at more than one person to get his way. No one would miss him, and those that did were just as bad as he was.

The thought of them searching for him, knocking at her door, made her smile and caused a shiver to move down her back. It would be wonderful. Like take-out. They'd come right to her door.

Her hands left him, and he dropped to the floor. The loud *thud* vibrated under her feet as she hummed low in her throat. Poe stepped over him as she swayed her hips, dancing to the song that played in her mind. Her hands reached up over her head as she closed her eyes, every nerve in her buzzing in that blissful way only feeding could bring.

She danced her way to the kitchen at the back of her house. The black stone floors were cool against her bare feet. She liked the way it felt. Like the cold battled against the heat that moved through her. The black stone tile was the same colour as her cabinets, dark with a bit of sparkle to it. It made her silver hardware look chilling in contrast and the white marble countertops look too bright. The lights turned on to their dimmest setting when she danced in, lighting the bottom of the cabinets against the floor and the white shelves that lined her black backsplash.

On the other side of the island, she pulled open her fridge — also black — and pulled out a bottle of wine. She pulled the cork out with her teeth and spat it across the room before she put the barrel to her mouth and took a deep gulp.

"Alexa," she called to her smart speaker. "Play my clean up playlist."

Somebody To Love by *Jefferson Airplane* started playing, and she jumped around, wine bottle clasped in her hand. She shimmied her naked hips around as she pulled the tarp she kept under the kitchen counter out and danced her way to the foyer where she left her guest.

She paused in the hallway, her eyes on a framed photo of a man walking downtown. His hair was set in waves that shone in the light of the sun, perfectly lined up to meet his stubble that covered a strong, square jaw and let his thick lips poke through. Taunting her. Forever calling to her.

Poe pressed her back to the wall beside the frame, looking at the photo from the corner of her eye. "As far as a meal went, he wasn't completely disappointing. But can a girl get a little help in the sex department?" she huffed. "I basically had to drive myself there."

Poe rolled her eyes as she brought the bottle back to her lips and caressed the edge of the frame with her free hand. Her nails were long and black, pointed at the ends to look like the claws she knew she deserved.

"You'd be so different, wouldn't you, Dex?"

He'd take good care of her, she was sure of that. She'd known him long enough to know he'd take his time. He'd explore every inch of her, find every button — and then push it until she was begging to meet her maker.

A sad sigh left her as her lips vibrated together.

Unfortunately, she'd never have him.

Poe shoved away from the wall and looked at the framed photos. Every one of the same person.

Dex.

Through every season, all over Toronto, she'd taken photos of him. Captured him from every angle. Whether it was on his way to work, playing a game of basketball, or at the grocery store, she had photos of him doing everything. Like she was a part of his life. Living his life right alongside him.

She would have had him already if that taste wouldn't be the end of him.

A low groan left her as she was filled with disappointment.

"So dumb that I can't have you. I mean, look at you, you're fucking perfect. Look at me!" she hollered over the music, gesturing down to her naked form. "I'd be perfect *for* you!"

Bent at the waist, she laid the tarp over her runner — an amazing woven find she found at a flea market for a whopping twenty bucks — and grabbed onto the man's ankles. It was effortless to flip him onto it, just like it had been effortless to hold him up when he was nothing but dead weight.

Her strength was one of the few things she could thank her parents for. Likely the *only* thing she would thank them for.

The ceaseless sex drive would be something to thank her mother for, the sensual succubus that she was, if it wasn't paired with the kiss of death of her father — a reaper. She needed both constantly. Orgasms that wracked through her and fed something in the depths of her that needed — craved — pleasure, and the taste of death. The feel of a soul captured in her hands to be devoured instead of delivered to Death and his waiting arms.

"But no Dex for me," she murmured to herself. "Nope. No sex god for little ole Poe. Because *somebody* had to get their rocks off and give birth to the biggest party pooper alive." She shook her fist at the air. "I'm talking to you, mom, you fucking slut. Couldn't just keep it in your pants with the reaper, could you?" She rolled her eyes, full of a lifetime of annoyance.

She looked down at the lifeless man lying on her tarp.

"I just have to settle for these fuckers. Men who are unapologetic assholes and don't give two fucks about my pleasure. So... thanks for that." She took another gulp of wine before she held up the empty bottle and frowned. "Hey, who drank this?"

Poe set the empty bottle on the bench against the wall, ignoring the shards of glass she swore she'd clean up later.

Her eyes settled on the man at her feet. "Wow... drinking all my wine too. So fucking selfish." She kicked him.

She took her time rolling him up in the tarp, her attention equally divided between dancing like her life depended on it, opening another bottle of wine, and conversations with the man she would never meet.

When he was finally all wrapped up, she flung him over her shoulder and pulled open the door. The cool air blew against her naked skin and she chuckled low under her breath. "Oops. Better not draw any unwanted attention to myself by strutting buck naked out into the wild."

She let him drop to the floor as she danced up the stairs to her bedroom to quickly get dressed. Her bedroom was just as gothic as her kitchen. Endless black with touches of white and silver.

Framed photos of Dex covered her walls in here too. Poe winked at him as she pulled on some yoga tights and a loose tank. She paused in front of the mirror, pulling her wild, shoulder length curls up over her head and securing it in a messy bun with a scrunchie from her dresser. She blew at the curly bangs that covered her brow before she lifted her shoulders at her reflection. "Gorgeous, as always."

Sashaying down the stairs, she scooped up the remnants of her meal and settled his weight on her shoulder before she shoved her feet into some runners. Her toes hooked around the door before she paused, shouting back into the house.

"Alexa... shut up."

Poe continued to hum to herself as she loaded him in the back of her Ranger and pulled the cover over the bed. Nothing like a long, relaxing drive after feeding. Maybe she'd pick up something on the way back, a little treat for herself.

She clicked on the radio and grinned as the same song played through her car stereo.

"Well, I'll be damned! Tonight feels like my night."

2

E VERY NIGHT WAS THE same. Another bar. Another Club. Anywhere where there was a crowd and people went out looking to burn off some steam. Usually the same steam she wanted to get rid of.

The club was packed. Bodies brushed against hers, unknowing of just how dangerous that could be. Unknowing of the reaper blood that flowed through her veins and itched when this many people were around her. Begged her to do something. To devour.

She wondered if that was just an affliction of her toxic blood. If maybe she would be normal if she only had reaper blood inside her. If she wouldn't look at all the people around her as something to claim, but instead would only receive a call, much like her father did. If maybe, succubus blood alone would allow her to fill her nights with endless pleasure without the bite that stole lives away. If she could orgasm without the souls that needed to coat her tongue, slide down her throat like an elixir made to soothe the ache in her.

Poe would never know. There was no way to go back and undo the mating between her parents. No way to assuage the tainted thing she was that wouldn't cost mortals and immortals alike their very breath. Their soul.

She wasn't a completely heartless bitch. She didn't just bring anyone back to her bed or foyer. Poe was selective. She tried to choose someone who smelt of something dark. Who had something sinister like a smoke that moved under their skin.

Sinful.

Greedy.

Treacherous.

She wasn't sure how she knew. Maybe she could thank her father for that. For being able to see past the smiles on their faces to the souls beneath. To see just how dirty their sins made them.

The bass of the music combined with the dim lighting and neon lasers that moved endlessly through the air was as intoxicating as the alcohol to most. Mortal drinks did very little to make her drunk, but they could cause a pleasant enough buzz if she drank fast enough.

Poe always drank fast enough.

She moved to the music, disappearing in the crowd like she was just like them. Mortal. Mundane. Bound by a short and unextraordinary life. Sometimes she wished for that. Being immortal wasn't always what it was cracked up to be. Sure, she got to live longer, but the endless routine of needing something to starve a craving that drove her closer and closer to madness felt... exhausting.

Yet, here she was.

On the hunt for one more. Just one more. Always just one more.

A firm hand wrapped around her wrist and yanked her back. It wasn't a strong pull, with her feet set apart, and had she been prepared, she could have easily stayed where she was. But Poe was three bottles of vodka in and she wanted to feel lost. She ignored the thrum of movement around her, which meant the pull moved her a little to where they wanted her to go.

Eyes opened, she stared at a beautiful woman. She had brunette hair that went down to her slim waist. Her eye makeup was perfection. Black lines that highlighted her eyes and eyeshadow blended in pleasing hues of pinks that matched her fuchsia dress. Anger did nothing to strip away any of her appeal.

Poe smiled at her. Her smile made a small knot appear between the woman's brows. "Where's Adam?" She shoved Poe, her hands planted on her chest.

Brow quirked, she pursed her lips in question. "I'm sorry, who?"

A pretty pink polished fingernail pointed up at her face. "My boyfriend, Adam. Don't try to deny it. People told me they saw you leave with him last night and no one has seen him since! Where the hell is he, you whore?"

"*If* I slept with your boyfriend, that would make me a whore? Even though I would have had no idea he was your boyfriend? And I owe you nothing? Can you explain that to me?" Humans were such silly things. Driven by their emotions — usually in the wrong direction. It made Poe wish she was a being who fed off jealousy. It was rampant and usually misplaced. She would forever be full.

"Are you saying you fucked my man?" She shoved Poe again.

Poe's eyes dropped to the spot on her shoulder where she was continually being shoved. If she wanted to, she could reach out and snap the woman's neck. Just a flick of her wrist and it would be done. Such fragile things, and yet they acted as though they were predators. "No. I'm saying your anger is misplaced."

"Where is Adam?"

Poe caught her wrist when she tried to shove her again. Her thumb ran slow circles over the woman's flesh as she pulled her into her chest. Poe was tall for mortal standards. Five foot ten to this woman's five foot two, maybe. Add in the three-inch heels, and Poe still towered over her. Her eyes heated as they bore into the warm brown eyes of the woman in her grasp. She felt her mother's magic move through her, saw the moment it seeped through the woman's skin and placated her.

"Who cares about Adam?" Poe grinned down at her. "Let's talk about you? What's your name?"

Her pupils widened as a grin lifted the corner of her lips. "Fiona." Her voice was trapped behind a dreamy haze as she stared up at Poe. "You..."

"I'm Poe."

"Adam..."

She shushed her lightly. "Who is Adam? He's not important. Are you as bad as he is?"

Fiona giggled. "I'm worse."

"Really?" Poe knew that was true. She could sense it on her. Could see the darkness, the torture that lived inside her, begging to be unleashed on the unsuspecting. "You're a bad girl, aren't you?"

"Yes." She reached up to caress Poe's cheek. Her bottom lip pulled between her teeth as she rose up on her toes, trying to get closer to Poe. "You're beautiful," she murmured.

"Yes, I know." Poe had the attractiveness of her mother mixed with the interesting pull of death from her father. She was gorgeous. She dared anyone to say otherwise. As Fiona grinned like a lovesick fool at her, Poe pushed her hair back behind her ear. "Want to get out of here?"

Her nod bobbed her head as she continued to gaze up into Poe's eyes. She knew they'd changed from their amber to a scarlet iced with silver around her pupil. As she pulled Fiona into her chest, Poe wrapped her arms around her middle. She liked the way the heat of her body felt, the scent of her perfume like a hot meal right out of the oven. Her hands slid down the front of Fiona's dress, pushed under the hem of her skirt to brush along the smooth flesh of her thigh.

A moan left her as Poe's fingers moved up to brush against her panties.

She was so warm. Lust came off her in a heady scent that piled on top of the alcohol in Poe's system and made her feel intoxicated.

Fuck, she smelt good.

Fiona's head leaned back on her shoulder as a gasp left her. "Tell me you live close."

"Close enough," Poe told her.

She shepherded Fiona out into the parking lot and loaded her into her truck. Fiona's palm pressed against the glass when Poe closed the door. It made her chuckle as she rounded the hood to the driver's side. She was such a needy thing. Hopefully, she would be a better ride than her boyfriend had been.

Fiona's shoulders bumped Poe's legs open. The heat of her mouth closed over Poe's core as her tongue explored her. She was a ravenous thing, devouring every inch of Poe like a meal that would be taken away if she didn't finish it quickly.

Poe's fingers tangled in Fiona's hair. Her head rolled back on her pillow as she clamped her eyes closed. She wouldn't orgasm, she couldn't, not without the bite she so desperately needed to appease her, but if she could, she had no doubt Fiona would get her there.

She took her time. Not needing to rush her exploration.

Her legs locked on the sides of Fiona's head and held her as she rolled and changed their positions. She pinned Fiona to the bed, her fingernails digging into the flesh of Poe's thighs when she stayed there long enough to make her struggle for breath. With a grin, she climbed off her, smiling when Fiona gasped.

Poe climbed down her and pressed her lips against Fiona's. She dipped her tongue in her mouth. Her stomach tightened and her pussy throbbed at the taste of her on this woman's lips.

Her tongue traced over her lips before she pressed wet kisses down Fiona's throat.

She knew how this had to end. Knew the bite she took would be the one that stole Fiona away from this world. That didn't mean she couldn't make this last night one to remember... if she could keep her memories after she claimed her soul.

Between Fiona's legs, Poe dipped her head and tasted her.

There was something about the taste of treachery. It was sweet beyond reason. A sweetness she should know would do her in, but indulged in anyway. One she knew an abundance of would cause a sickness, but she was already sick. There was no cure for her affliction, so instead, she gorged herself on it just the same. She couldn't know what someone without sin tasted like. She'd been too righteous to have a taste. Too worried about what a single taste would mean.

As forbidden to her as her happiness.

Fiona squirmed beneath her skilful hands. The metallic taste of her so similar to blood, Poe would be so bold to say she preferred it. Like the way it teased at the parts of her that wanted just that. Wanted to sink her teeth into the smooth, flawless flesh of her shoulder and take all Fiona had to offer.

Why wait?

A bite was a bite, no matter where she placed it.

Her fingers dipped into Fiona's core and were immediately coated with wetness. Poe would bet her life that dipshit Adam had never fucked Fiona the way she deserved. Even the most blackened soul deserved to be laid out. To be wrecked so fully by waves of ecstasy, they thought they'd drown in them. What else made this wicked world worth living in?

Fiona screamed as her hands wrapped in the sheets. Her back arched off the bed. "Poe," she screamed, her voice as thoroughly worked as Poe made sure Fiona was.

"You like that? You like that, you filthy fucking sinner?" Poe asked before she closed her mouth around her again. The flat of her tongue pressed against her clit, rough like a cat's. The tip of her long, forked tongue dipped into her opening, coated in the intense flavour of her orgasm. Salty. Rich. Wild.

"Yes," she screamed. "Fuck yes!"

"Adam never ate you out this good, did he?"

"No," she admitted easily. "Never."

And no one ever would again. Her tongue dove deeper into her core, hitting that place inside her Poe knew would maker her see stars. Fiona bucked under her, her heels ground into the bed as she tried to scurry away, the orgasm too intense.

Poe forced her to ride it out before she sank her teeth around her. The tangy taste of her pussy mixed with the intoxicating taste of her blood before the light and airy taste of her soul filled her, spiced with sin. Fiona bucked once more before she sunk back into the bed. Poe's tongue slowly pulled out of her, coated in her juices as she sucked down the remnants of her soul. Crumbs of her creation.

Pushed up on her hands and knees, she looked down at Fiona.

She still looked beautiful. Fiona's hair fanned over Poe's pillows, her hands still fisted in her black sheets. Her head was slumped slightly to the side as she stared down at Poe with brown eyes that had lost all their warmth. Her dull flesh was still rosy along her cheeks.

Just what life had she lived that made her taste spiced?

What had she and Adam gotten up to together that painted their souls in harsh strokes of obscurity?

"Alexa! Play my clean up playlist!" Poe called as she climbed off the bed.

Bad Reputation by *Joan Jett and the Blackhearts* started, and she hopped off the bed. She held her fist in front of her mouth as she belted out the first few lines of the song, her hips shimmying to a beat she knew well. She danced her way into the ensuite, pulling a tarp from below the sink before she winked at herself in the mirror. She paused, wiping the blood from her bottom lip.

Her hair was a mess around her head. Poe wrapped a curl from her brow around her finger and let it bounce back into place when she released it. Throwing her head back, she sang the song at the top of her lungs, making Alexa fight for her robotic life to be heard over her as Poe turned on her heel before she dropped into a split.

Damn, she had moves.

She laid the tarp next to Fiona and rolled her onto it before she danced over to her closet and pulled on an oversized t-shirt and some panties. Back at the side of the bed, she picked Fiona up while looking over her shoulder at one of the countless photos framed on her bedroom wall.

"She was a good lay," she told Dex. Though she still had that sexual itch in the pit of her stomach that had yet to be satisfied. She should have flipped, put her pussy back in Fiona's face as she bit her.

What had she been thinking?

Poe chortled. "I wasn't thinking." Still, the hunger in her belly had dissipated some. It wasn't as demanding. She could wait until tomorrow, do things right.

With a pull of the tarp, she adjusted Fiona on her shoulder and strut from her room. She spared her bed a single glance, satisfied with the lack of mess. She wasn't a messy eater — unless she was.

She'd be a messy eater with Dex. She'd let him coat her in cum only so she could lick it all off.

The thought made her groan low in her throat as she licked her lips.

If only.

"Soon," she whispered to a photo of him as she passed it, even though she knew it was a lie. She would never have Dex. She couldn't. Not when she knew it would end in him on a tarp thrown over her shoulder, only to be placed in the bed of her truck while she drove out to the cemetery.

It was a clever place to hide bodies. On top of those already buried. A fresh grave was best, but an older cemetery worked just as well. One with no visitors. She could sense the absence there. Like the souls didn't bother to visit anymore because there was no one left to see.

Humming to herself, she shoved her feet in her boots and made her way out the door.

"Alexa! Shut up!"

3

HE DIDN'T KNOW WHY he did this. Why he followed this mysterious woman to the cemeteries night after night. Watched as she dug up the graves only to throw a tarp covered body atop whoever rested there.

She sang at the top of her lungs like the night belonged to her. Like she didn't have a place in her heart for the fear that would fill most as she desecrated a grave in the middle of the night. Something that was a felony in most places. It was in Toronto.

He wondered if she knew that.

It sure as hell seemed like she didn't care.

She danced around to music he couldn't hear. Dirt smeared on the pretty brown skin of her face as most of her curls were secured in a haphazard bun on the top of her head that leaned to the side, the rest fell in curly bangs over her brow. She was tall, toned. She had wide hips and thick thighs and a soft middle he enjoyed looking at when she wasn't covered in the massive t-shirt she wore now.

She was peculiar.

He could smell the immortal blood in her, but couldn't place it. She was likely a mix. A little of this, a little of that. As rare as that was.

It was crazy to think she'd been following him around for years. Maybe longer. It took him over a year to notice her snapping photos of him. She wasn't subtle. He'd been nervous at first, unsure just what she could want from him. When she did nothing but follow him around collecting photos, he decided she was harmless.

Dex had pissed off his share of immortals in his life. He thought maybe someone had come calling. Seeing her doing this, night after night, made him realize she wasn't really the type to do things for other people. She wasn't a hired hand, sent to follow him around. He wasn't sure what she was.

With the body buried, she tossed the shovel over her shoulder, spread her arms out, and dropped into a squat. She threw her back out, jerking her ass around.

A smile broke out on his face.

She was unhinged. This woman was, quite literally, dancing on people's graves. Why did that make him smile? It filled him with a humour he hadn't felt in a long time. She paused next to a headstone, laying her palm on it as she bowed her head.

"Sorry, old guy," she murmured to herself.

Dex's grin bordered painful.

She offered the headstone a salute before she spun on her heel and headed back to her truck. Dex watched her go. She was unkept chaos. She danced around the overgrown path, hand held out. Every so often, she swung the shovel at nothing and shouted into the night.

She enraptured him.

Sometimes he lay awake at night and wondered what she was doing. If he was the only person she followed. His heart sped up at the thought of being the object of her desire. Her love, as twisted as it likely was.

Not all love was the same. Some was dark and wicked. Some was as dead as he was.

She tossed the shovel into the back of her truck, pulling the cover over the bed before she climbed behind the wheel. Her radio jumped alive when she started it up. Loud and booming, it ate up all the silence in the night air as she threw her truck in drive and peeled away from the body she left behind without a care in the world.

Dex stood there, his eyes glued to the red lights on the back of her truck until they disappeared into the darkness. He stood in the night, the graveyard more a home than his condo downtown. The grave soil called to him. Damp and welcoming. He stepped back into the cemetery. His feet carried him over the hollowed ground, his body heavy with fatigue as it willed him to rest.

Not here.

If he rested here, he may never get up again.

He moved back to the fresh soil and dropped to his knees. His hands dug into the dirt, pulled it past him as he undid all the work she just did. Uncovering the body she worked so hard to bury — as much fun as she seemed to have doing it.

The tips of his fingers dipped through the dirt and brushed against flesh, still slightly warm. He wrapped his hand around her wrist and used it to lift the body out of the grave. He thanked the goddess of night he followed her over a year ago. That she was someone who could make his life easier, even without knowing.

Night after night she delivered bodies right into his waiting hands. A task that used to make him feel like a scavenger, often forced to take bodies that were rotting and filled his mouth with bile.

Perhaps it was best she never approached him. That instead she watched him through the lens of a camera. It kept her from seeing the monster he was.

His stomach churned, and he felt saliva fill his mouth.

Arms wrapped around the body of the woman she delivered to him, he held her in a hold much like an embrace. He revelled at the way the slight warmth of her body felt like a furnace against the chill of his own. He pressed her bare chest against his, the skin of her back smooth beneath his fingers.

How treacherous a thing he was.

His face dipped between her shoulder and neck as he inhaled her.

She smelt sweet. The sharp tang of salty sweat mixed with the fruity scent of a perfume quickly fading away, the stench of death too powerful for it to keep its hold. This was a scent he would always want to live in. Death brushed over with the heat of life. A scent straddling the line of two very different realms. Two very different gods.

Dex squeezed her as thoughts of the woman who just drove away filled his mind.

No, it was best they never met.

Safer for her.

As much as he knew that was true, there was a yearning in the depths of his belly unlike any he'd ever felt before. One he knew he wouldn't be able to reason away. Wouldn't be able to starve off. It was as desperate as the one that filled him now as he inhaled the woman in his arms.

A hunger.

Dex snarled as he sunk his teeth into the flesh of her neck and ripped it away. He barely chewed, the flesh sliding down his throat before he bit into her again.

He was a monster.

And he was always hungry.

His blunt nails scraped against the white of the windowsill as he heaved his weight up through the window. The twisted part of his mind thrilled at the invasion. At the disruption of privacy, and the crack in a safety she likely thought couldn't be so easily broken.

Monsters had a way of getting into the most guarded places. Hiding under beds, making the shadows in someone's bedroom home.

Dex set his feet silently on the floor and wished he'd been gifted with eyes that saw through the darkness. That he could lift the veil of night from the room and see more than the silhouette of her in her bed. The gentle rise and fall of her under her sheets as she fell deeper and deeper into the arms of the sandman.

Lucky bastard. He got to hold her in a way Dex never could.

The taste of blood and flesh filled his mouth as he crossed the room. At the edge of her bed, he could see her better. Make out the line of her face, the pillows of her lips, the thick curtain of her lashes as they rested against her cheek. The mess of curls that was usually as unkempt as she seemed was hidden from him, under a dark bonnet, the details of which he couldn't make out in the dark. Her hand was thrown up over her head, the other tucked into the front of her panties as one of her legs escaped the confines of the sheets.

She was so beautiful. Fascinating in her stillness. So close to the dead in sleep. Just a breath away, really.

Dex reached out a hand. Even in the room's darkness, he could see the blood that coated his hands up to his wrists. He leaned over her bed, his hand hovering over her face. How easily he could eliminate the small space between asleep and dead. He needed only to lower his hand. To cover her mouth. To steal the deep breaths she took.

His hand closed into a fist at the thought.

So beautiful.

He stepped away, not trusting himself so close to her as those thoughts filled his mind. As the image of her throat between his teeth wrapped an invisible thread around him, pulled taut as it tried to get him to close the space. To succumb to the thought not fuelled by hunger — his belly was full — but by something else. Something more thorough.

Something he didn't understand.

Slow steps carried him across the room to the chair by the window. He sunk down on it, his eyes on her silhouette as he timed her breaths. Made sure she took them. One after another. Made sure she stayed among the living, knowing how treacherous it was to be torn from that place before someone was ready.

How that curse caused an ache in his bones.

Dex leaned back, his elbows on the rests as he folded his hands under his chin. Watching was its own kind of pleasure. Knowing how easy it would be to cross the room and steal her away. From this room. From this house. From this life.

No.

He couldn't.

Shouldn't.

His leg bobbed as his foot bounced quietly off the floor. Hunger had always been a driving force in him, one he knew better than to fight. It was a war he would always lose, a battle that would leave him broken and begging for a solace that would never come. This infatuation was new. This craving he didn't know how to satisfy.

He wanted to taste her as much as he didn't. Wanted her flesh in his teeth, her blood in his mouth, but he also craved it just where it was. At home wrapped around her bones while his hands explored her. Marked her. Made her scream.

Dex's eyes narrowed in the dark as time ticked on. Until the smell of morning made him look to the window at the darkness he knew would soon be chased away by the sun.

She'd been a relief. Someone who gifted him with all he needed without realizing. He couldn't help wonder if she could gift
him with all he wanted too.

He held the sigh in his chest as he rose to his feet and crossed
over to the window.

To take her would be to dive into an ocean of misery he'd
never be able to swim out of. Held under the surface as the
water filled with a sorrow he'd carry with him. To leave her
would be trying to stay afloat while a storm waged.

That's what it felt like lately — this engouement with this
mysterious, peculiar, wild woman. It felt like trying to survive
a storm that tore at the foundations in his chest, threatened to
wash his cold, dead heart away in a flood of — what? He wished
he knew.

A single step, he decided. He needed to take a single step and
see where it led him. An introduction she could take or leave.

Dex threw his leg out of her bedroom window, gazing back
at her over his shoulder. She was his. As much as he was hers.
She'd dug him out of a grave he'd resigned himself to forever be
buried in.

Fuck, he mentally cursed.

This couldn't end in any way that would be good. For either
of them.

He was a monster, and all he could do was take. He just hoped when he was through taking what he wanted, there would still be something of her left besides ruin.

4

POE

THE WEIGHT OF HER camera felt at home in her hands as she followed Dex up Yonge Street. He looked all kinds of sexy today, with his fitted white t-shirt that put his broad shoulders and muscular back on display tucked into fitted black denim shorts that ended well above the knee.

The little slut. With those buns fresh out of the oven on display, like he didn't know exactly what he was doing.

She lowered her aim and snapped a few shots of his ass. Never know whether she might need them later.

He strut through the crowd with an air of confidence some would call swagger. The warm brown of his skin was alight in the sun's gleam, making it look brushed with gold. Vibrant. Alive. Wondrous.

Poe kept her distance as she walked down the street behind him. She leaned against a storefront, scrolling through her shots when he went into a coffeeshop. He was in there a while, long enough for her to debate crossing the street so no one noticed her. She was someone who drew attention.

She could thank her mother for that.

Poe mentally shook her fist in the air and cursed her mother.

With an adjustment of her weight on her feet, she gauged the traffic. It was always heavy on Yonge, there weren't a lot of streets that allowed drivers to turn off unless it was a sidestreet. She wasn't about to walk a block north or south to the lights to cross, and unless she had a death wish — which, some days, she did, not that it would matter anyway — she wouldn't be able to cross through the heavy traffic.

Her lips pursed, and she blew air through them, making them vibrate.

What to do? What to do?

Before she had to come up with her answer, Dex came out of the coffee shop with two coffees in hand. He reached onto his head, shoving his sunglasses back down onto his nose.

Fuck, he looked good.

Probably tasted a million times better.

No. No, Poe. You can't taste him, you freaking horn dog.

She rolled her eyes at herself, hating that she couldn't. He would be so freaking good. Tall, dark, and handsome. Built like someone who could toss her around until she begged for him to give her just what she wanted. What she craved.

Hopefully, he denied her.

Nothing good would come from him giving her what she wanted — at least not for him.

Dex stood outside the coffee shop, his eyes on the surrounding crowd with two cups of coffee in his hand.

Her stomach lurched as a frown turned down the corners of her mouth. She wondered just who the hell he was getting coffee for. It bothered her there was anyone in his life he thought he ought to grab a coffee for.

Some buff, sexy dude that could hold Dex down and take what he wanted while Dex begged for it, or maybe some slinky woman who could climb him like the tree he was. After all this time, she didn't really know his type. She hadn't seen him with anyone, couldn't gauge the company he kept.

Or who he'd be buying coffee for.

Dex turned.

Poe tensed, his gaze right on her as he lifted the cup and placed it on the sill of the coffeeshop window.

What the fuck?

Her feet were glued to the spot as he turned and continued his way up the street. Poe waited until he was the right distance ahead of her before she walked over to the coffee he'd left behind and picked it up. She turned the white cup, looking it over.

There, written in marker, was a little note.

For my sexy stalker.

Well, damn.

She held the cup in her hand, letting the heat of the coffee warm her palms, rivalling the heat from the summer day. Blowing air through her lips, she watched as it lifted the curls on her brow. And here she'd thought she was being so stealthy.

Dex noticed her.

Bringing the coffee to her lips, she sipped it. A slow sip. Just a taste.

Black.

Hmm, she pursed her lips in thought.

It was an easy order. No fuss. There was no way for him to know it would be just the way she liked it. He didn't know her.

Maybe not, but he *noticed* her. As Poe sipped at her coffee and slowly followed him up the street, camera abandoned to hang over her shoulder, she wondered just how long he'd known she was following him.

Thoughts of her interaction with Dex made her feel like she sleptwalked through the rest of her day. She couldn't make sense of it. Didn't know what it all meant.

Where to go from there?

The immediate answer was obvious. She had to go out. Find someone new to feed her. Hopefully without the edge of hunger that made her blood too hot and her chest feel hollow and wanting, she could figure out just what to do with the sexy man who had taken up so much of her life the past few years.

Dressed to the nines, like bait on a lure she knew would catch her just what she needed, she went out on the town. She'd lose herself in the carnal need that drove her and then she'd had the brain space she needed to further wonder what her interaction with Dex meant.

She hoped.

Fuck, she hoped.

Pain sliced through her scalp as her neck was whipped back, her hair tangled in someone's grasp. Her feet came out from under her as a hand wrapped around her waist and lifted her off her feet. Her hand covered the hand in her hair. A man's hand, she could tell by touch alone. It had thick fingers, a brush of hair along the side below his little finger.

For a split second, she wondered — out of all the people she'd done away with — which demon had finally come searching for her. There were countless possibilities, which meant no one immediately came to mind as he pulled her back into the alley next to the club she was hoping to enter and threw her up against the brick wall.

She collided with brick so hard it rattled her teeth.

Damn, he was strong. She liked that.

A grin stretched across her face as her curls curtained her eyes, her chin slightly down as she looked up at him. He was tall, not as muscular as her Dex, but he looked like someone who spent his time in the gym well. His tanned skin told her he enjoyed the summer sun, and the product that held his hair slicked back from his brow told her he was someone that took pride in how he looked.

Fair. He was attractive enough.

He pressed his palm against the wall next to her head and leaned into her space.

Poe leaned forward, inhaling the musk of his cologne and the scent of darkness underneath it. It was thick, heavy. She dragged her tongue over her bottom lip as it took over her senses.

"Where the fuck are Adam and Fiona?" he hissed.

"Who?" *Oh, you know. Just buried a tad shy of six feet under.*

His hand wrapped around her neck, and he slammed her back into the wall. Her skull slammed off the brick, making her ears ring. Her grin widened as the pain radiated through her skull.

"Don't play with me, little girl."

Little girl? Poe rolled her eyes. "I'm far from little," she defended.

His hand cracked across her cheek. "I'm not going to ask you again."

He would. They always did. This tough guy was no different from any other. He made a lot of noise hoping it would scare her, make her cry. Covered in snot, she would tell him exactly what he wanted to know. Only she couldn't because Adam and Fiona weren't buried together and once she undug one grave — well, who's to say they wouldn't start digging them all up?

It was a slippery slope, and her balance wasn't all that great.

The sharp tip of her fang tore into the flesh of her cheek and the metallic taste of blood filled her mouth. It made a jolt of energy surge through her, tempted the part of her that craved the taste of death that came after.

His grip tightened, and he leaned into her space. Hot breath blew across her lips. "Where are they?"

"I thought you weren't going to ask again," she chuckled.

He slapped her and released his grip on her throat.

Poe crumbled to the floor, the tight hem of her little black dress riding up. She felt the humid night air on the bottom of her ass cheeks, the heat of the pavement against her bare thigh. Her hand lifted and pressed against her throbbing cheek. She spat on the floor by his feet before she glared up at him, a smile on her face. "You didn't ask for my safe word."

"Are you out of your fucking mind?" He squatted beside her, his hand once again circling her throat as he lifted her face up to his. "What are you, high or something? Your eyes are all kinds of crazy."

She was sure they were. He'd awoken a craving in her, and she needed to feed it. "Or something."

He lifted her slightly toward him.

Her palms left the pavement as he dragged her lightly across it, the painful bites of cement against her thighs enough to make her tingle. "Who are you looking for again?"

"Adam and Fiona," he hissed, full of barely kept anger.

Poe pursed her lips in thought. "Hmm, doesn't sound familiar. I meet so many people."

He shoved a phone in her face, a photo on the screen. "Well, maybe this will jog your memory. We know they left with you. And ain't no one seen them since."

"Is that right?"

"Yeah, bitch. That's fucking right."

Bitch. Was he serious? There were so many better insults. Bitch was so tired. If she had a dollar for every time someone called her a bitch, her piggybank would be close to bursting. Was it too much to ask for a little creativity? She could think of so many amazing insults to throw at him. He was a bowl of dirty dildos. A cum sandwich. A discarded tampon. An anal pimple. This guy was a shit-eating beaver.

Poe chuckled.

"What the fuck is so funny, bitch?"

She rolled her eyes. "You."

His fist connected hard with her cheek, making her see stars. Lucky for her, night was her favourite time. She loved the stars. She let them dance around her head, stealing her vision as she swayed, that smile of hers still in place.

Her eyes opened when she felt something cold push under her chin, lifting her face. The familiar sound of a gun being cocked filled the air and their eyes met. His were blue, but not bright. A blue that was covered in a light fog, hidden away. As shadowed as he was deep down. Her eyes danced between his, his face so close to hers, she was surprised their noses didn't bump together.

"You got a death wish?" he threatened, though the gun would likely be enough for most people.

A low hum left her throat. "Most days. Unfortunately, I doubt any reapers would deliver me." She dropped her voice to a whisper. "Apparently, my dad is a big deal."

"Is he now?" He shoved the gun harder into her face. "I don't think he's a big enough deal to save you from me."

If only he knew how ridiculous that sounded.

"Now's the time to talk. If we leave here, I won't give you another."

"Leave?" Poe considered his words, the vision of unbothered. "Where to?"

He got to his feet, his hand wrapped forcefully around her upper arm. He yanked her upright, the gun still pressed up into the sensitive flesh under her chin. "It'll be your last resting place."

Poe blew out a breath, making her lips vibrate. "Good thing too. I'm mighty tired."

Annoyance burned bright on his face as he released her to pull something from the back of his jeans. He removed the gun from her face long enough to secure a silencer to the barrel. No sooner was it attached, he fired a shot into her thigh.

Her muscles tensed, and a searing pain radiated through her leg. Her weight fell back against the wall as a laugh bubbled up from her chest. It was slow at first. Quiet. It rose and rose, maniacal, as she flicked her eyes up to meet his puzzled stare. "It's *buttercup,* by the way. My safe word."

"Next shot goes between your eyes," he warned.

"And here I thought you were taking me somewhere," she pouted. "Alright, alright. I'll take *you* somewhere. To see your friends. Adam and Fiona."

Getting shot wasn't her favourite kind of torture. It was lazy. Just as lazy as the names he threw at her. It was strong arming someone when you needed to play them skillfully, like a fiddle.

Couldn't he see she was someone who needed to be played skillfully?

Sheesh, this wasn't her first go at being tortured. He could at least put in more effort.

He stepped toward her, menace in his eyes. "Are you fucking with me, little girl?"

"Yup, but I'll take you to your friends just the same."

A forceful hand wrapped around her upper arm, and he shoved her further down the alley toward the opposite end. He hustled her into a large black SUV waiting for them at the end, and she once again rolled her eyes at the lack of originality.

Poe yanked the hem of her dress down over her ass as she strut toward the vehicle as though she didn't have a bullet lodged in her thigh. Each heeled step, one that would carry her toward the end of a runway instead of this brute's car.

She let him manhandle her into the passenger side before he rounded the hood. He climbed in, hard eyes on her. He threw the car into drive and ripped out of the parking lot.

Silence surrounded them, and Poe reached over and clicked on the radio.

His hand shot out and connected hard with her cheek, sending her flying into the window. Her temple hit the glass, and she was once again immersed in stars.

He clicked the radio off.

"Well, aren't you a charmer?" Poe smirked. "You really know how to show a girl a good time."

The scent of his darkness surrounded her, thinning her saliva and making her throat dry. She'd take him to see the bodies of his friends, right before she dug him a hole right alongside them.

5

POE

HER BARE FEET HIT the chilled earth as the handsome brute pulled her from the car. Her heels were long abandoned. She had no use for them anymore, and they pinched her toes anyway — as cute as they were. He jerked her arm, making her stumble into him as the glare he wore since they met bore down at her.

"Fuck around and I have another bullet with your name on it."

Mortals were *so* boring. "Yeah, yeah." Giving him a taste of her strength, she pulled out of his grasp and whirled on her toes. She waved his words away, letting him know just how much impact they had on her as she walked down the slight hill toward the two tombstones she carefully selected for the people she was feeling better and better about biting. If those fuckers were in league with this asshat, she'd chosen correctly.

Thanks dad! That whole reaper sight thing really helped me choose the right souls to devour.

A hum vibrated up her throat as a song popped in her head. She swayed her hips as she made her way through the rows of headstones to the two she sought.

Amber Lee Gibbons and *Chase Arnold Mewls.*

They weren't close to one another. Amber had been buried far off in the corner of the cemetery. The area was more crowded, and far too many headstones had chunks missing. The plaques in the earth had names the world had worn away. Their names as forgotten as the people buried beneath it.

Chase was buried under a tree. A fallen metal rusted bench sat under it with two legs that gave out. Grass and weeds climbed up the metal, making it its home. It was a peaceful spot. Poe could imagine a loved one sitting on the bench and wasting hours chatting to the grave that housed nothing but bone and rotting flesh.

If souls could go wherever they wanted, why the hell would they want to spend their time in this depressing scene?

Depressing to some.

Poe quite liked it.

She skipped the last few steps over to Chase's grave — a grave he now shared with Fiona. The muscles in her thigh tensed and her leg gave out, but she quickly caught herself twirling with her hands in the air. "And she stuck the landing," she grinned.

He didn't smile. She was beginning to wonder if he could.

"So serious," she muttered. "Who died?" A cackle escaped her as she gestured around, pressing her palm to her brow. "Oh yeah. Right. Just everyone here..." And the people this stern handsome man was looking for.

Rounding the headstone, she bent at the waist and folded her arms atop it. She blew her bangs from her face before she looked up at him.

"Well, here we are."

A knot appeared between his brow. "What?"

"Fiona." She pointed to the grave, the earth freshly shifted. "I liked her a bit better than Adam, but it definitely wasn't a *love at first sight* kind of thing. She had the same bark as you and," she scoffed. "Boring."

He pulled the gun from the back of his belt. He aimed it right between her eyes. Confusion warred with the rage that churned inside him. "What the fuck are you talking about?"

"Fiona." Poe lifted an arm and waved a hand around her head. "Busty brunette. Gorgeous face. That jawline." She whistled low. Fiona was a looker. It was too bad. She could have spent another night or two in the sheets with her. She really put in the work.

"You *killed* her?" His eyes were wide, torn between looking at the grave she led him to and the woman responsible for it.

"Yep. And Adam, but he's back there. Not a great spot, if I'm being honest with you." She shook her head. "Someone did *not* love Amber Lee."

He ran his hands through his hair. "Dig it up."

It was her turn to be annoyed. He'd dragged her away from the club, where she hoped she could feed both her lust and her need for a soul. It was an inconvenience. Then he'd shot her in the leg. It was pain without even the indication pleasure would come, but now she had to dig. *Without* her soundtrack or a full belly?

He was plain rude.

Hip cocked, she stood and crossed her arms under her chest. "Um, no."

"No?" He pointed the gun at her, driving the fact that he could shoot her again at any moment. "Does it look like I'm playing with you?"

Poe lifted her shoulders. "Not in any way I'm enjoying."

The answer she gave was not the one he wanted. The silent *pop* of his gun filled the air, louder than it should have been. It echoed in her ear as her hands dropped and covered her stomach. Numbness overcame her, the scent of death and grave soil a tempting concoction, reminding her of the roots firmly planted inside her. She fell to her knees. Her eyes dropped to watch the dark blood seep between her fingers as she huffed out an annoyed breath.

This was not ideal.

Her weight slumped to the side as she dropped to her ass, her legs folded beside her, feet cupped partially under her butt as she bared her teeth at him. "That was rude."

Ignoring her, he picked up a shovel and dug.

Poe watched him, a little proud that he had to dig up the corpse of his shitty friend all by himself. That's just what he deserved. No, what he deserved was for her to jump at him. Leap into the hole he was slowly digging — *honestly, put your back into it* — and sink her teeth into him. Suck his soul right out of its casing. *That* was what he deserved.

Her nose lifted as she inhaled the scent of him. Of his soul. She'd seen her mother do this before, but she wasn't sniffing for lust. It was so peculiar to see how her magic crossed the lines. She didn't have the magic of her mother, or her father, instead she had something twisted between. As tangled and perverse as she was. Devouring souls instead of delivering them. Craving a lust that could only be appeased when she sunk her teeth into the flesh of the person it came from. With the taste of lust filled her along with the tang of their blood and a hint of their fear.

She wished he were afraid. Just a pinch of fear could really add a bit of flavour to the hottie she was quickly learning was an absolute asshole.

He shot her.

Twice.

With absolutely no foreplay.

What a fucking weirdo.

The heat coating her fingers was soothing. A steady stream of life she struggled to hold on to, made all the more dramatic by the chill of damp soil under her ass. Her eyes dropped to look at the black dress pooled around her hips. She really wasn't dressed for this. This was an activity that required her boots, and if she had the choice, she probably would have chosen something white if she was going to be bleeding. It would be so beautiful watching the scarlet of her blood devour the white fabric.

She smiled at the thought.

What a dark and beautiful sight. So like watching life slowly ripped from someone's eyes. It didn't happen all at once. It was slow. Something that took its time. It felt like she could live in the moment for an eternity, and then a single breath cut the thread securing that moment and it was gone. *Whoosh.* Just like that.

Breathtaking beauty.

Literally.

Poe laughed. It shook her shoulders and caused a pinch of pain to move through her stomach with each shake. The taste of blood filled her mouth as the unhinged sound escaped her.

"Would you shut the fuck up, you crazy bitch?" he huffed, out of breath. As muscular as he looked, he didn't seem like he was in shape. She could dig that grave in her sleep.

Fucking amateur.

She heard his shovel hit wood, and a growl erupted from the hole. "Is this a fucking joke to you? Do you think this is a game? You do realize I will kill you, right?"

"As fun as meeting Death might be, it's not in the cards for me. What are you threatening to kill me for now? I already told you I killed Fiona..."

He tossed the shovel out of the hole and it landed next to her. His hands dug into the dirt as he climbed out. A few strands of dark hair escaped the product holding it back, making him look completely dishevelled coupled with the dirt smeared over his face and forearms.

This guy was extremely dramatic. He climbed out like a beast that needed to be leashed. Teeth bared and eyes narrowed as he scurried out of the hole and stalked toward her. He fumbled with the gun in his belt, losing his hold on the menacing look before he aimed it at her again.

"Where is she?" he spat through his teeth, practically rabid.

"Huh?" Poe forced herself to her feet. She walked past him, ignoring the gun pointed at her, and looked down at the coffin in the hole. Oak. Definitely not the colour she would have chosen for herself. Why not just a pine box? Black and sleek was the way to go, obviously. What was the point in anything else? It was the limousine of coffin colours. If you were on your way to meet Death, you should do it in style. Did these people know nothing?

She shook her head of the thought, remembering what she was supposed to be looking for.

Fiona.

She was *gone*.

Her brow cocked as she grinned. "Well, this is interesting." Dead bodies didn't just get up and walk away. Well, usually. She supposed there were some instances where they could, but there was no scent of necromancer magic in the air, no witch's mark. None of the obvious indicators that was what happened.

So what did?

Poe turned just in time to catch the shovel hurled at her.

"Enough games. Dig them up. I'm not fucking around."

The urge to sink her teeth into his neck was put on the back burner. She was going to. Boy, was she going to. She was going to do it while he was kicking and screaming. Without the calm her succubus magic could bring him. The joy. The lust. The pleasure. No, she wanted him squirming under her hands as she devoured his soul. Terrified and in pain. But she also wanted to know if Adam would be where she left him.

Lifting her shoulders, she ignored the tinge of pain in her leg and her stomach. It would be gone soon enough. She made her way over to the sad resting place of Amber Lee and set to work. She hummed the tunes she usually did as she quickly dug through the earth. Far faster than the pitiful man who stood watch, gun in hand, as though it could do something.

The whole thing reeked of SDE, if she were being honest. Small Dick Energy. Not that Poe ever wrote anyone off for size, but this guy, she just knew he had no idea how to use it. Just *jack hammered* his way to the finish line, the poor person beneath him holding on for dear life and counting down the moments until it was over.

Just like Adam.

Sad.

Fucking mortals.

Her hands slipped over the wood handle of the shovel, a coat of blood on her fingers. She watched it paint the handle. Erase the colour of the wood and cover it in the scarlet she loved so much. The shovel hit wood, and she tossed it haphazardly behind her.

For a moment, the vision of the shovel soaring through the air and hitting her captor in the throat filled her mind. The sharp blade would slice through his jugular. Eyes wide, he'd gasp for air, look around for help, all the while Poe would be in the hole — unrealizing of how close he danced to Death's door.

She smiled.

If only.

Her life felt full of *if onlys* lately.

"Soon, soon, soon," she muttered to herself as she dropped to her knees and brushed her hands over the dirt below her. "Soon I'll have a taste of him and see if all that assholery adds any flavour to that blackened soul. It had better... otherwise, he's not really worth the trouble."

"What are you going on about?" he barked from above.

Poe ignored him as her hands brushed over the wood.

"Huh." She sat back on her heels and looked down at the coffin below her. This was most definitely a simple pine box. "No love for Amber Lee," she muttered with a shake of her head.

"Well?"

So demanding. "He's gone."

"What do you mean, *he's gone*? You've been messing with me all this time, haven't you? Wasted my whole damn night out here chasing ghosts. I'll show you. I'll show you just who you're messing with."

Poe ignored him as she pondered.

She may not always be on the ball. There were days where her scatter brain made her giggle until she was out of breath. When she searched for her phone for an hour, only to realize she'd been using it as a flashlight in her hand the whole time, but she knew where her bodies were buried. Fiona and Adam had been in these graves, company she'd gifted to Chase and Amber Lee, company she'd wondered if they'd enjoy on her drive home, or if they'd be angry about the uninvited guests.

No one liked an unexpected drop in.

So, where the hell were they?

Fisting the loose soil in her hands, she lifted it to her nose.

"Are you listening to me?"

She wasn't.

The familiar scent of death was there, as soothing as always. She inhaled past it, to the decay, the smell of worms and damp earth, to the blood and flesh beneath. To the hunger.

Interesting.

Pain radiated through her shoulder, then her back. The raging man-child emptied the clip into her back while he screamed and shouted.

Whoa, tantrum much?

Annoyance made her hop out of the grave. She tackled him to the ground and grinned at the horror that transformed his face.

"W-what the fuck?" he stammered.

Poe clicked her tongue at him. Her thighs settled beside his stomach as she straddled him, holding him down with a strength she hadn't yet showed him. Blood leaked from the wound on her shoulder onto his face.

Drip, drip, drip.

He blinked each time it hit his cheek as she leaned over him, her hands wrapped around his wrists as she pulled them up and above his head. He tried to fight it, but it was no use. She was past annoyance now. The immortal part of her, dark and ravenous, wanted something for all the pain she gave him. She never gave her pain away for free.

"You should be dead! What the fuck are you?" His feet kicked against the floor as he tried to buck against her weight, but it was no use. He was no match for her, he never was, but she wanted to let him earn what she was going to do to him. Sign his name on the dotted line for a punishment that came with no promise of redemption.

Poe dragged her nose along his cheek, smearing her blood across his skin. "I'm the consequences of your actions, *little boy.* I'm the cry of all the people who screamed *no* into your ear, finally given a blade to wield against you. I'm the weight of your sins made real, and I'm hungry and unforgiving. And all those sins you've marked yourself with without consequence, those are what feed me... and tonight..." She dipped her nose, tracing the line of his lips with the blood smeared there. "I know they'll feed me quite well."

Her hand wrapped around his chin as she forced his face to the side.

"No. Stop, stop! Wait! W-wait, just listen to me for a second, would you? I have money. We can just—"

"Money?" Poe laughed as she ran the tips of her fangs over the sensitive flesh of his neck. "I wonder if you'll offer him money, too."

"Who?" he whimpered.

"Death." She sunk her teeth into him.

6

HE THOUGHT THE COFFEE would have been invitation enough, but she continued to follow behind him for blocks, sipping her coffee with question in her eyes and her camera around her neck.

It was as adorable as much as it was frustrating.

He'd been torn. Half his walk was spent kicking himself for being so bold as to reach out to her, knowing he would do nothing but ruin her. He spent the rest counting the minutes. Counting down seconds in hopes the next one would be one where she caught up to him and introduced herself.

Not that she needed to. He knew who she was.

Poe Wiley. As far as he could tell, she was unemployed, though she lived her life like she was comfortable. She spent her nights in the city. Going from restaurants, to bars, to clubs. Bringing people home with her.

That caused a pang in his chest he tried to ignore as he rubbed his hand against it and dropped to a squat on her porch. He looked around, the darkness of night shrouding him like a child she welcomed into her bosom. His lock pick kit in hand, he let himself into Poe's home. Tonight was different. A step into her life that required a door instead of a window.

She should be there.

Normally, she'd have someone in tow by now. Someone she would load into the back of her truck and drive to their final resting place — well, final as far as she knew. His sexy, quirky little serial killer. A serial killer by mortal standards. Immortals had a different set of rules and laws. Especially where dark and shadow beings were concerned. Her scent was most definitely dark.

He closed the door quietly behind him, basking in the aura she left behind.

The heels of his boots clicked off the dark hardwood of her floors. He sunk his hands into his pockets, placing his lock pick in there as he made his way further into her home. It felt a little like walking into a dark cavern. The dark colours and lack of light, the butterflies that flit anxiously in his belly, warned him of impending doom.

A long hall stretched out before him. There were two entryways two metres in from the doorway. The one to his left looked to be a laundry room with a doorway that led out to her garage, the other led to a living room area. He ignored both and walked down the hall.

He paused. A pretty row of black twelve by sixteen frames with eight by ten photos in them decorated the walls, leading the way deeper into the house caught his attention.

The thought of staring at her photos, seeing into her life, made him giddy.

It was — *him.*

Every single photo.

Photos of him on the street. At work at the morgue. Coming out of his condo on Bremner. Having coffee on Lakeshore.

Intrigue brought him further into the house.

He knew Poe was following him. Enough for him to want to look into her. See just who she was and what she would want from him. What he hadn't expected from his sexy little stalker was this level of obsession. There were no photos of anyone or anything else in her home. Every frame held a photo of him.

It was different from seeing a wall where photos were tacked up. Taped. She had taken her time with each of these. Printed them off and put them in a frame.

It was sweet.

Dex smiled as he ran a finger down the edge of the frame. He'd never been so proud to have his photo taken. A thought struck him, and he quickly backtracked through the hall to the stairs.

He wanted to see her room. Wanted to know if he took up just as much space in there, in the intimacy of her bedroom, where she likely brought all those people she buried later, as he did through the hallway downstairs.

The thought thrilled him. Knowing he was there in some small way to bear witness to whatever happened there.

The first room was a guest room. It was impersonal, like a showroom at a furniture store. The second was an office, everything in gothic decor. The third was the one he searched for and he couldn't keep his grin from taking over his face as he stepped in and looked at the collection of framed photos at the head of her bed.

He was here.

In her bedroom.

His feet carried him to her bed as he kicked off his shoes and climbed on. Head at the end of the bed, he crossed his ankles and folded an arm behind his head as he pictured them both here, wrapped in the dark sheets, as photos of him stared down at them.

Fuck. He was screwed.

No. No. He could rein this in. He could be just like her. He could watch from afar. Capture her and keep her in little frames that decorated his home. Make her a part of his life without taking a bite out of her flesh, devouring her until his hunger sated and he could pretend to be human again.

The smell of her seeped into his nose, and a low groan escaped him.

Fuck, she smelt good. Delicious.

No, Dex. No.

His hand sunk into his pants as the smell of her surrounded him. He undid the button of his dark jeans, shoving them open as he fisted his erect cock in his hand. The smell of her was too strong. It filled every inch of him, pumped all his blood down to the throbbing cock in his hand.

Closing his eyes, he summoned the image of her.

That look of confusion that caused that little knot in her brow as she looked at him, a mess of curly black bangs on her brow, the rest of her hair pulled up in a messy bun at the very top of her head as her slender, brown shoulders soaked up every bit of sun that summer day offered. Her black tank hung loose on her chest, dangerously low under her arms, where he could see the small mounds of her breasts peeking out from the thin fabric. He wished the fabric would shift ever so slightly, and give him a peek at her dark nipples.

Fuck.

Dex pumped his hand over his cock. His thumb pressed against the small slit, rubbing through the bead of moisture there so he could paint it over his shaft.

Her thighs were thick. They rubbed together, making her shorts lift slightly higher into her crotch. Pulling his eyes there. She stood with her large camera in her hands, dark eyes on him.

"Did I confuse you?" he grunted. "Did I confuse you just as much as you confuse me?"

He did. He knew he did. Dex saw the look on her face. The face that was always a bit wild, her eyes unfocused. There was a madness there, deep-rooted. Like she was conjured from it. Brewed in a concoction of dark intention and mischievous misdeeds.

Her lips parted in his mind, and she moaned.

Fuck, that moan.

He'd make her moan just like that. No, he'd make her scream. First in ecstasy as he filled her to bursting, shoved his cock so deep in her needy pussy that she couldn't take it anymore. Bit down on the flesh around her nipples until the taste of blood filled his mouth, and she begged him for more. Always more. She'd always want more with him. He'd make sure of it.

How long could he hold on to those screams until they twisted and became ones that haunted him? Until the nails dug into his back became her last defence?

A groan left him as he pulled up his shirt and came on his stomach. His balls lifted as spurts of seed decorated him. Poe still moaned in his mind.

He couldn't have her.

That thought soured the moment.

A groan of frustration left him as he threw his feet to the floor and dragged a hand through his cum. He got it all, collected it as he walked over to her pillow and smeared it over the black fabric. He stood there, looking down at the piece of him he'd left behind for her as he tucked himself away, did up his pants and sighed.

He wanted her more than he'd wanted anything in his long life. This life or the one before.

He was screwed.

Poe was screwed.

Loud, slightly off pitched singing stole his attention. Dex flipped the pillow before he quietly left the room and made his way toward the sound.

"Alexa, play my rage playlist!" Poe called as she slammed the front door behind her and stalked down the hall. Dex watched her from the top of the stairs, covered in dirt and blood. She tore off her little black dress. The fabric fell to the floor in tatters as she stood there bare, chest heaving.

Fuck You by *Lily Allen* played through several smart speakers. He heard the song come from the back of the house where he figured the kitchen must be, the living room, and her bedroom upstairs.

"Fucking stupid mortal men!" she bellowed, arms fisted at her sides.

Rough night?

Her curls fell to her shoulders, but they were matted with dirt and blood at the ends, the hair clumped together. His eyes narrowed as he looked at the blood smeared over her middle, her leg and her shoulder.

Was it hers?

It didn't look like there were any wounds to go along with them. Poe turned in the full length mirror by the front door. She held onto her shoulder as she inspected her back, looking for something.

Dex leaned over the bannister, as curious to see if there was anything there as Poe was.

Satisfied by what she saw, she stalked toward the steps.

He tensed, quietly stepping away from the banister and scurrying down the hall to her bedroom. He didn't know why he hid from her. He fully intended on letting himself be known. Finally introducing himself to the stalker who captivated his mind as easily as she captured his photos.

With the door closed over, he peeked through the barest space he left himself.

Poe's grime covered feet hit the top of the steps and she lifted her arms above her head. Gyrating her hips, she threw her head back and sang along to the song that played. Her fingers dug into her hair, giving it a good shake before she hopped in place. Arms held out, she spun.

His cock thickened again in his pants as he watched her.

She was as haunting as she was beautiful. Covered in destruction and chaos. Brown skin brushed over in dirt he knew was from a grave, held fast to her skin with blood so rich it made his head spin as she continued to dance. She skipped down the hall toward the bathroom across from where he hid. She threw the door open with reckless abandon. The door stopper vibrated as she slammed her hands on the light and strut in.

Dex waited until the sound of the water ran for several minutes before he crept out of her room and crossed the hall. He peered into the bathroom.

Poe was in a large clawfoot tub. The tub, the sink, and the toilet were the only things in the whole bathroom that were white. The rest of the room was — unsurprisingly — black. Dark tiles covered the floors and the walls, continuous. It made the room look both massive and small. It was disorienting. The ceiling was white. A black chandelier hung in the middle of the room, with electric candles instead of bulbs.

A hum came from the woman sunk shoulder deep in the water. Her leg stretched straight up as she ran a dark washcloth over her shin, that adorable knot between her brows.

"What an insufferable man," Poe spoke to herself as she washed her leg all the way up to her black polished toes before she returned it beneath the obnoxious amount of bubbles and lifted the other. "With his gun waving and heavy hand. Like damn. Buy a girl dinner first, am I right, Dex?"

He tensed.

The fuck? How the hell did she know he was there?

Poe chuckled, her attention straight ahead of her. "Very rude. You wouldn't do me like that, would you, Dexy?"

He opened his mouth to speak.

"I know you wouldn't," Poe answered for him before he could.

Brows dropped, he leaned a little further into the room. A chuckle trapped in his chest when he saw the massive framed photo of him on the wall at the foot of the tub. It was a heavy, ornate black frame. The image was of him topless getting out of the sauna at the gym.

How the hell did she even take that?

She wasn't talking to him, not really. Still, happiness moved through him at the thought that she spoke to him like this. Included him in her day.

"I didn't even get the relief I needed for all my trouble," Poe pouted. "Ah well. Ain't no one as skilled at playing this pussy piano like I am." She reached behind the tub and opened a black box.

Dex leaned in, forever intrigued by this woman.

Poe pulled out a thick dildo. She admired it before she pressed a quick kiss to the veiny shaft. "You'll take care of me, won't you Dex Jr.?"

Fuck me. He swallowed back the groan that threatened to escape him. She was going to be the death of him. With his eyes squeezed closed, Dex leaned his brow on the wall beside the bathroom door. He called all his willpower to keep himself from strutting into that room, snatching that poor imitation of his cock from her hand and lifting her onto his own.

The sound of the suction being attached to the side of the tub made his eyes snap open.

Fucking hell...

"And who is this? Did you bring a friend?" Poe sang.

He closed his hand over his crotch where his own swollen cock waited. He had her friend right there. Peeking around the corner, he watched Poe on her knees in the deep tub, a vibrator in her hands.

Yup, she was going to kill him.

Poe shoved her fingers in her mouth, letting them dance over her tongue before she ran it over the dildo attached to the side of the tub. She scooted back, positioning it right where she needed before she held the rim and backed onto it. Her mouth fell open, and a sigh escaped her. She rolled her hips, her rhythm quickly making water slosh around in the tub.

He was captivated. Her small breasts swayed, her nipples decorated with little bars with skulls. Her nipples were the same dark brown he imagined they'd be. Pebbled and perfect.

A click of a button started a whirring, and Poe held the vibrator in front of her face, inspecting it with mischievous eyes before she dipped it under the water.

Pleasure transformed her face. Her rhythm quickened with the vibrator pressed against that sensitive bud of flesh he desperately wanted to take into his own mouth. Wanted to squeeze between his teeth until she squirmed within an inch of her life, until she coated his face with her pleasure.

Dex slipped his hand into his pants. He couldn't believe he was ready again. That the mere sight of her like this could so easily rattle him. Make him want to test his willpower when the warm flesh of her was in his grasp.

He timed his pumps with the sound of sloshing water. Imagined it was him behind her, his hand wrapped around her as he twirled that pebbled nipple between his fingers. Tugged at it, made her scream his name.

Fuck, he wanted her to scream his name.

"Dex," she moaned, obliging the dream he begged for but never dared thought he'd be so easily given.

His hand sped up as he watched her. His cock was as desperate as it was for another release as it was to find it inside her. To fill her to bursting with him, to watch as he pulled his cock out and his cum dripped from her. Marked her. Made her his in a way she couldn't deny.

He couldn't either.

Dex held his breath as it quickened, the sound of the water sloshing out of the tub onto the floor combined with her low, throaty whine enough to carve a jagged nail across his mind that let madness seep in. That's all madness ever truly needed, a single crack. His mind was full of cracks. He supposed that made him a little bit mad.

Of course it did. No sane person would have broken into Poe's house and jerked off on her bed, only to follow her into the bathroom to do it all over again. As she called out his fucking name like an invitation he knew he had to deny.

For her.

Her fangs pierced her bottom lip, and blood rolled down her chin. Her mouth opened, head thrown back as black smoke wafted from her parted lips.

He came. Hard. His chest heaved as he felt his cum squirt out of his cock and hit her pretty black walls. His brow dropped, questions danced in his mind as the image of dark smoke pluming from her mouth filled his head.

Another sigh left her. "Sure beats being shot."

Rage filled him. He forgot himself. Cock out, he rounded into the bathroom and crossed the room to the tub. His hand wrapped around her upper arms as he lifted her slightly from the water, eyes roaming over her freshly cleaned skin.

"Someone shot you?" he barked. "Who? I'll tear the flesh from their throat while they choke on their blood."

Surprise flickered over her beautiful face before the corners of her mouth lifted. Her hands wrapped around the rim of the tub as she turned into him, her face tilted up to meet his. "Dex," she whispered low, her voice still thick with lust.

His name from her lips almost made him forget his fury. *Almost.* Dex wrapped his hands around her arms, made sure he had a good hold on her, before he hoisted her from the tub. He set her feet on the black mat, waited until they were steady beneath her before he turned her to examine every inch of her exquisite body.

"Someone shot you?" he demanded the answer from her.

"Mhmm," she nodded. She let him hold on to her, but kept pressing her bare chest up against him. The warm water beaded on her flesh quickly soaked through the thin fabric of his dark t-shirt with each brush of her body against his.

As far as he could tell, there wasn't a mark on her. He released her arms to trail his hands down over her skin. Her arms, her abdomen, her legs. He left no inch of her unexplored by his fingertips, turning her to thoroughly examine her back.

There was a ghost of wounds along her back. Lightened flesh, not quite scars, or maybe scars that had been lightened under the hands of Time.

"Don't fret, they'll be gone after my next feed." Her head cocked slightly to the side as she thought about it. "Technically I already fed, but unfortunately my mother is a silly hoe, and my father is a careless bastard, and the result is me having to deal with a hunger that needs... double the satisfaction." She lifted her shoulders. "You could say I fed one beast, but not the other."

What was she talking about? "Who did this to you?"

Poe's lips pursed. "Hmm. I didn't get his name. It didn't seem overly important."

"You'll bring me to him so I can..." He tried to think of all the things he wanted to do to the man who harmed her. His mouth salivated with countless thoughts of just how he would make him pay. How slowly he'd do away with him. Until there was nothing left but a torso and head as he screamed apologies that would never be enough.

"Can what?" she asked.

"Can kill him," Dex told her. "Slowly."

"Oh, well. I already did that. Not the slowly part though. I killed him a lot faster than I would have liked, but I was already dirty and there was the whole *being shot* thing. These humans and their bullets."

His hand traced the slight scars. "But you're fine."

"Better than fine."

She was *fine*. As happy as that made him, it wasn't enough. Someone shot her. Someone shot Poe, this beautiful, twisted, wicked thing before him. That couldn't be forgiven. He wanted to make someone pay for it, even if she claimed she already did.

"Where did you bury him?" Dex asked.

Poe shoved her tongue in her cheek as she continued to look up at him through her lashes. "Does it matter?"

It most certainly did. He wanted to dig him up, devour every inch of him until there was nothing left. No piece of that bastard that could desecrate the land where they buried him. "Yes. You'll show me," he demanded.

"After," she cooed.

"After what?"

Her hands wrapped around his wrist as she turned in his arms. His anger seeped through his grasp as his eyes took her in, so close he could smell the scent of passion and death coming off her in waves. It made his blood hotter than should be possible as she stood on her toes, so close she breathed against his lips. "After you kiss me."

Dex's heart jumped to life. The physical feeling of something that had often hung dormant in his chest suddenly beating startled him. It had been so long since he felt the sensation, it was hard to breathe through. It hammered in his chest, a caged thing determined to break free. He swallowed hard, but his hand cupped under her chin, his thumb slowly tracing the line of her bottom lip. "Kiss you?" his voice was raspy as he spoke, his throat suddenly too tight.

"Mhmm." Her lips brushed lightly against his.

The brief touch of her lips against his fogged his mind, filled him with thoughts of having her in just the way he wanted. He needed to taste her lips, inhale her breath. See if the warmth of her tongue could heat the frigid temperature of his own.

"Dex..."

"Yes," he groaned.

"You broke into my house."

"Yes," he admitted.

"You watched me bathe."

He was helpless to do anything else. "Yes."

Her dark eyes dropped to where his cock, already slightly thick in her presence, hung out of his pants. "Just what were you doing in my house, Dex?" she asked. He didn't miss the teasing tone she used. It wrapped around his heart and ceased its beating.

"I painted the walls outside your bathroom door with my cum."

Poe lifted her face, inhaling deeply. "Did you?" There was no disgust worn on her face, none in her voice. She looked pleased by the admission. Her hand dropped and wrapped around the length of him. Her fingers barely touched around the girth of him as she squeezed.

Dex's eyes closed, his head fell back. "Fuck," he hissed.

"Were you marking your territory?" she questioned.

"Would you consider yourself marked if I did?" It pleased him to think it would be that easy. That she could consider herself his because of the liberties he'd taken there.

Her hand jerked up his length, and he groaned in his throat. "Look around. I'd say you marked me well enough already."

A chuckle left him as he dropped his head and let his nose bump against hers. "You haven't been marked by me, Poe. If you had, you'd feel the sting of it. The hurt it leaves behind."

"Are you going to hurt me, Dex?" That grin he loved so much painted those pretty lips.

"Yes," he admitted. "And you're going to love every minute of it."

7

POE

HER NIGHT — CLOSER to morning — was certainly turning around.

Dex tasted a thousand times better than she dreamt. Like hot fires that burned out of control. Like cold winds that cut past her skin and made her ache, made her burn in its own way. The pain a kind that sliced through her flesh down to her bones. He was an explosion of spice that sent her senses into overdrive, made her tongue push out past her lips, desperate for another taste. He was floating and falling. That weightless feeling as she plummeted way past everything right down to the wrongs she knew would curl her toes. It was hell, glorious and welcoming in the way it damned her. In the way, it marked her like the very souls she wanted to devour.

He pulled her hand from the impressive length of him as he shoved her across her bathroom, turning her until she planted her palms on the counter between her twin sinks. Dex tangled his hand in her hair, his blunt nails scraped sinfully against her scalp as he lifted her face and forced her to watch their reflections in the large framed mirror.

The rough feel of his calloused palms against the round globes of her ass made her shudder in anticipation. "You've been playing an awful lot of pretend, Poe," Dex growled.

Had she?

It didn't feel like she had. She kept herself busy. Far too busy to play games. Just what did he mean?

"Calling out my name while you play with yourself, instead of letting me do it." He leaned his weight forward, his hands covering hers. The heat against her back was insatiable. It awoke that part of her that hadn't been fed since Adam but was famished and begging.

Poe wiggled her ass into him. "I let you do it all the time."

The rough stubble of his face rubbed against her cheek. He ran their cheeks together, his eyes glued to hers in the mirror, before he dropped his face to the space between her neck and shoulders. He inhaled her like a hearty meal, his tongue tracing a damp line against her skin.

His tongue was cold. An ice cube pressed into her flesh, her skin pebbled with each slow drag. His hands were chilly too, though not as frigid as his tongue. Her back arched, the thickness of him gliding between the dampness of her ass cheeks, still wet from the bath.

"I wonder just how you'd taste," he whispered against her skin.

Poe didn't miss the hunger there, it was a hunger she felt too. "You would have no reason to wonder if you had a taste."

Dex angled his hip, the thick head of a cock she longed for knocked at her entrance, and she had every intention of letting him in. Letting him fuck her until she forgot about how desperately she wanted to sink her teeth into him, breathe something poisonous and life ending into his veins. She wouldn't — *couldn't*. Not when she'd finally gotten him within her grasp. She wanted to keep him for as long as she could.

Savour him.

"One taste would be a taste too much," he warned.

How true that was. One taste would be all she got if she wasn't careful.

Dex's fingers laced between hers, folding under her palm as he slowly pushed forward. "Is this what you picture when you snap photos of me? Is this what you picture when you ride that imitation of a dick in your tub? Me sliding into you, just like this?" he asked.

How tame this was for all the things she pictured. "Maybe at first."

She felt herself stretch around him. She was so full, her breath filled her chest as she waited to see just how full he could make her as he slid inside her inch by glorious inch. His free hand wrapped gently around her throat, lifting her face to be sure she kept her eyes on his in the mirror. "And then?"

Dex was dark intrigue. His brown skin was warm, making her wonder if his roots were just as blended as hers. The wide set of his nostrils and the thickness of his lips were much like hers, as was the brown of his skin. His waves hinted at textured hair without the product he'd used to keep it in a style that suited him. The thought of what he was bounced around in her head as his scent moved over her. Intoxicated her as thoroughly as the cock that filled her did.

It was cold too, she realized. Not freezing, but not the heat she usually expected when someone was between her legs.

The question of what Dex might be flashed in her mind for a second, but it was gone when he bottomed out inside her, the head of his cock pressed against a button that made her arch her back, her head falling back on his chest.

Dex pulled out, the movement so torturously slow Poe lifted onto her toes and clenched her walls, trying to hold on to him.

"Poe," he hummed her name.

"Hmm?"

"And then?"

And then? What were they talking about?

Dex stalled with only the head of his cock inside her. "Poe."

Her eyes opened, and she looked up at him. A defiant little frown wrinkled her brow as she let her feelings on his pause of movement be known. She wanted to feel him. Wanted the brutality she knew was barely leashed inside of him let loose on her. She wanted her world rocked so hard, the ground cracked beneath her feet and she tumbled in. Swallowed whole.

"And then?" he repeated.

She wiggled back, but he stepped away. Just enough to keep him from pulling out or going in any further. "Don't tease me," she warned.

"I think you'll quite enjoy being teased by me."

Fuck, she didn't doubt it.

"Tell me about your fantasies, Poe. It seems I've been a part of them for quite some time." His hand slid down her throat. The feel of his chilled flesh on the heat of her own made her shudder. His thumb and finger grabbed hold of her nipple, yanking it until she let out a strangled yelp.

He shifted the bar through her nipple but didn't lighten his hold, his grip merciless as he rolled her perked bud painfully between his fingers.

She sucked in a laboured breath.

"Tell me," he demanded.

A whimper left her as her pussy throbbed with need. He was right there, the tip of him inside her, and she was being denied. The succubus in her wasn't pleased. She was the one that was supposed to make him feel this way. Supposed to fill him with an uncontrollable need that made him rut her the way a girl deserved. With her feet behind her head and sweat on her brow.

Tell him.

If only she could summon the thoughts.

"You're always so rough with me," she started, thousands of hours of pleasurable material playing behind her eyes as she clutched them closed.

"Am I?"

"Yes," she moaned.

"How?"

How? If she had to tell him that, it would take away most of the fun. "How about you show me what you can do, and I tell you what you need to work on?"

His chuckle vibrated through her back. His hand yanked on her piercing in a way that bordered on pain but was erased by the pleasure that followed. "I assure you, there's nothing I need to work on."

As long as she'd longed to hear his voice, she was tiring of it now. She wanted him to use his mouth for other things. Words could come later. "Prove it."

Dex scooped her up so quickly a squeal escaped her. Hand behind her knees, he carried her into her bedroom and tossed her on the bed. She bounced, her head hitting the pillows and a grin on her face. He was a magnificent sight. Tall, wiry, broad. Muscular, but not built. Fit enough to toss her around, which was all that mattered. Taut flesh shone warm brown in the dim light, the length of him bobbing against his belly with each step he took toward her.

Poe licked her lips.

His eyes traced the movement. "Did you want a taste, love?"

She liked when he called her that. It sent jolts of something through every inch of her. She wished he meant it. That he had the same hole in his heart she did that only he could fill. That he was desperate to have her. Keep her. Make her his. "Yes," she admitted easily. She did want to taste him. Wanted the thick length of him to fill her mouth until her jaw ached. To push back in her throat until her eyes watered and the taste of salt assaulted her tongue.

Poe tingled in anticipation.

"I think I want a taste of you first."

Getting to her knees, she shook her head. "I've waited so long for this... give me a taste, Dex."

He stood at the side of the bed, watching her. Hunger flashed in his eyes.

Rolling onto her back, she hung her head off the edge of the bed and opened her mouth. She let her magic slip, her forked tongue breaking past the barrier of her lips to be put on display for his approval. Surprise flashed through his eyes for a single second. A tingle of glee moved through her when he stepped into her, the head of his cock bumping against her lips.

She shifted, heels planted on the bed as she waved her knees opened and closed.

"A taste for a taste?"

"Gods, yes!"

Dex stepped into her. The length of him slid past her parted lips as he bent over her. His hands wrapped around the back of her thighs as he sealed his mouth over her flesh. A moan was trapped behind his cock as it bumped the back of her throat. He tasted of salt and sin. Of paradise when she stood outside the gates, knowing she'd never be allowed in.

She moaned with her mouth sealed around him, her tongue licked up to press against his flesh right above his cock as she swallowed and made her throat grasp the head of him. He tensed, and she knew he was as good as gone.

She was damn good at this. Decades of experience led to an unrivalled skill. Lucky for him.

The flat of his tongue moved through her as her toes curled against the bed. Each rub of his tongue, each tease of his teeth, each gasp around her made her plummet head first toward a release she wanted to chase but also wanted to run from. She wanted this to last. Wanted hours to pass with the taste of him on her tongue, the feel of her mouth on his cock.

They devoured one another like the monsters they were. Leaving no inch of them unexplored. No flesh safe from the feel of their teeth or the gentle hurt of their bite.

A guttural groan left him when her lips hit his balls and she breathed her hot breath around him.

"Fuck." He pulled his cock out of her and spun her around. "I need to be inside you. Now."

"So impatient," she teased as he pulled her ass to the bottom of the bed and settled his hips between her thighs. He held the length of him in his hand, slapped the underside of his cock against her clit until she gasped.

"You have no idea."

She did, because as much as she teased him, she was impatient too. She wanted to feel the stab of him inside her. Wanted to be impaled on him.

He slapped her again with his cock before he moved it through the moisture he created moments earlier with his mouth. It glided effortlessly through. The feel of him moving through her folds and against her clit made her lift her hips, urging him to enter her.

"Dex, don't tease me."

"It's hard not to when I see how desperate you are for me." Despite his words, he sunk into her.

She was so full. Her teeth chattered as the cool feel of him registered. There was no heat to the cock inside her. It was a sensation she wasn't prepared for. She didn't have the time to question it. His hand wrapped around the hair at the crown of her head, tugged her head back, and he thrust into her.

The pace was quick. The wooden legs of her bed scratched against her floor and her headboard banged against the wall.

His nose dragged along the length of her neck, her back arched as his thrust made him slam off her in the most delicious way. This didn't feel like sex — she'd had enough of it to know it well. This felt like she'd been infected with her own lust. Like she didn't need the bite of death that haunted her whenever anyone was between her legs. Whispered of what she needed to take.

It clouded her mind and filled her to bursting.

It felt celestial in a way. Like something divine touched a hand to her chest and rid her of all her afflictions. All that was left was the primal need to mate. To ride him until neither one of them had the energy to do anything else.

Her fangs tingled, but not wanting the taste of a soul, but something else. To mark him. To leave something people could see that told this and every other realm he was hers.

What the fuck?

Her orgasm banged at the door, and she was hard tempted to let it in. She'd never had an orgasm without the bite she needed to go along with it. Without the taste of death on her tongue.

What was happening?

She was about to come, and hard. That was what was happening.

No, this couldn't happen. He was hers. He was here now, finally, after all this time, and he was hers. She couldn't do this. Couldn't succumb to the need she knew she would, to the hunger that drove her. Not if it cost her Dex.

Her Dex. Her handsome, sweet, big cocked, hands like a god sent to undo her every knot and tangle, Dex.

Toes curled against his chest as he slammed into her. Her ass bounced up to meet him, thrust for thrust, as his hands planted on the back of her thighs pushed her into the bed for the bed to push her right back to him. The tempo made her breath catch in her throat and her eyes roll back.

Fuck, this was so good.

But she couldn't.

Her pleasure curled up in her lower belly like a snake ready to strike. To snap at him. To release a venom she knew he would never come back from.

Panic made her eyes snap open as she looked up at his face. Watched the lines between his brow deepen as he huffed out a breath, as close to the edge as she was.

So close to his demise.

There was nothing she wanted more in the moment than to keep him, so she did the only thing she could. She braced her feet on his chest and pushed.

A little too hard.

Dex flew off the bed, across the room, and slammed into the wall. Framed photos of the man in question shattered to the floor as he slumped down onto her dresser and it crumbled under his weight.

Poe fumbled to get upright. She crawled quickly to the end of the bed, her fingers curled tightly over the edge as she looked at the chaos she created. The black paint was cracked, bits of plaster rained down to join the broken frames and dresser, and Dex sat in the middle. His eyes were narrowed at her as he pushed some of the decor she had on the dresser off his legs and slowly got to his feet.

"Well, that was..." He turned, showing her the enticing taut ass she wanted to sink her teeth into. A small piece of glass impaled one of his juicy cheeks and he sighed as he wrapped his hand around it and pulled it free. The blood was red sludge, coagulated and thick. It didn't drip off the glass as it should. He tossed the glass down onto the rest of the rubble before he stepped out of it and flashed her a grin. "Unexpected."

Poe cleared her throat. She did her best to avoid the question in his eyes as she looked down at the mess on the floor. "You broke my dresser," she said flatly.

His steps paused halfway to the bed as he looked down at her incredulously. "Technically, *we* broke your dresser."

"No." Poe shook her head as she got to her feet, her hand planted on her hips. "*You* broke it. With your body. You just..." She gestured to the mess on her floor. "Crushed it!"

As sexy as he was, he was a bit of a bull in a china shop. He just destroyed absolutely everything he landed on. How much did he even weigh?

Poe strut over to him, wrapped her arms around his waist and lifted.

A startled grunt escaped him. "What are you doing?"

She held him off the floor for a second before placing him back on his feet. "A hundred and... ninety-three pounds."

"What?"

"It's no wonder you broke all my stuff." She stepped back and looked him over. Aside from the slight butt impalement — not particularly how she would have chosen to impale him, but those plans would have to wait for another day — he looked pretty unaffected by her rash decision to launch him off her.

His finger cupped under her chin and lifted her face up to his. "I'd say it was likely a combination of my weight and the strength in which it was thrown across the room." He pressed a light kiss to her lips, question in his eyes. "May I ask *why* you launched me across your bedroom?"

Her eyes dropped to his erect cock bobbing between them. *Needy, attention seeking thing.*

"Because of that." She gestured to it. "Put it away."

"It was *away* before you shoved me," he grinned.

"*Ha, ha.*" That was actually pretty funny. Poe covered her eyes with her hands. "I'm not talking to you about this until you put that away... not in my vagina... and buy me a new dresser."

The heat of his lips pressed against her own and her knees went weak. She kept her hands where they were as his tongue dipped playfully in her mouth, just enough to tease her, before he pulled away and chuckled low in his chest. "That sounds fair. You're a bit off your rocker, aren't you?"

"A bit?" Poe snorted. "I'm a lot off my rocker."

She listened to the sound of him moving around her bedroom, hoping with everything in her he was getting dressed so she wouldn't be tempted to mount him again and ride him to his ruin and her sorrow.

"Good." He gently removed her hands from her face and she looked up at Dex, fully clothed and grinning down at her with those fluffy, kissable lips. "I quite like it."

8

DEX

THE LAST PLACE HE expected this night to take him — especially when he'd been balls deep in the most beautiful woman, immortal or otherwise, he'd ever set his eyes on — was IKEA. He wanted to be back in her bedroom, making her come until she couldn't see straight, forgot her name, and was nothing but a mess of limp limbs and constant smiles on her bed.

Time abandoned them. He wasn't sure when, but by the time they climbed into her truck, it was early morning. The sun crested the sky, lighting it with hues of pinks, yellows, oranges, and purples. She was mostly quiet, casting Dex accusing glances as she murmured under her breath about never being able to find another dresser for the sixty bucks she found that one for.

All his reassurances he would pay whatever he wanted were waved off. He could tell this had nothing to do with the dresser and a lot to do with something she wasn't quite ready to tell him.

Yet.

They stopped at a cute cafe for breakfast, a meal as quiet as the car ride. It felt like the morning dragged on as he felt anxious nerves in the pit of his stomach waiting for her to tell him what was going on, just like it felt like it flew. Before he knew it, there they were, walking around a furniture store.

As soon as they stepped foot through the automatic doors, the grey cloud over her head lifted and took Dex's anxiety with it.

He tried not to question it too much. The thrum of his heart, the butterflies in his stomach, and the anxiety she caused in a body that hadn't felt any of those things in so long, he couldn't remember the last time he had. It should bother him more, but with her hand in his, all his bothers were chased away.

Poe tightened the grip she had on his hand as she pulled him through the showrooms.

Butterflies flit around his stomach as she ran her thumb along his.

Okay, this wasn't *entirely* a bad time.

Who was he lying to? He loved it. Loved walking beside her instead of having to discreetly look over his shoulder to be sure she was still following behind him. Loved the feel of her hand in his, the way she kept grinning up at him as she pointed over to a couch in a bright yellow and scrunched up her nose in disgust. He loved the way she always seemed to have a skip in her step, a fuel behind her movements. A constant excitement in the most mundane of tasks.

Loved — *her.*

No, he didn't. That was crazy. They'd just met.

He only broke into her house the night before, ignoring all the reasons why he shouldn't, but they'd been a part of one another's lives for years. He'd felt her every day. Watched her little quirks as she made her way through the city like it belonged to her. To him, it did. She was this energy that couldn't be ignored. That she thought for a second he wouldn't notice her following him around was ludicrous. How could he not?

"Why are we looking at couches?" Dex asked when she let go of his hand and plopped down on a velvet green couch. His hand closed into a fist at the absence of hers, suddenly ice cold without her heat. "I thought I was here to replace the dresser I broke."

"Ah!" She pointed an accusing finger at him. "Finally fessing up?"

He grinned and plopped on the couch beside her. "Yes. It was terribly rude of me to crush your dresser. My apologies."

"It was," she agreed. "But you're forgiven."

"Ah." He touched a hand to his chest. "Thank goodness. You had me worried."

Poe slumped against him, her head on his shoulder as she peered past her curls, those dark eyes captivating him. "Meh. I don't really hold a grudge. It takes too much energy. I have to remember who, and why, and where..." She held her hands up, counting on her fingers. "Best to just kill them if they *really* piss me off."

Dex's eyes went around the room to the mortals looking for furniture. It was early and there were more people than he thought would be out and about. Luckily, no one paid them any mind. Those who did likely thought Poe was joking.

Hopefully.

They sat there, completely unrushed. He listened to the soothing sound of her breathing, the warmth of her body leaned into him a paradise he wished he could endlessly live in.

Her hand ran lightly down his thigh. "How's your ass?"

"I've been told it's perfect," Dex joked.

She whirled at him, her hands clenched on his thighs. "Who?"

Dex lightly traced her jaw, staring into the fire in her eyes. "Are you going to kill them?"

"Maybe."

He sighed. "Then, I'm afraid I can't tell you. Not until you tell me just why you — *I*—" he quickly corrected. "Broke your dresser."

Poe kept her eyes on his, challenging him for a moment before she huffed and got to her feet. She held her hands out, wiggling her fingers at him as she waited for him to take them.

Helpless to deny her, he took her hands and let her pull him to his feet. Her hand wrapped around his, fingers laced, as she lightly dragged him out of the sofa room. "Fine, I'll tell you while we look at dressers."

"Deal."

After going in the wrong direction, grabbing hot dogs, and spending way too long lying in display beds, they were finally in the showroom for the dressers. Poe walked around, opening drawers and slamming them with way too much force, as she hummed to herself, completely ignoring the deal they made before they left the sofa room.

Dex stepped forward as she pulled out a drawer, catching it before she slammed it shut. "Care to have a chat?" he asked.

"What about?" she inquired as she opened another drawer.

He chuckled. She was adorable. Just a scatterbrained, chaotic mess that captured his heart as easily as she threw him across the room. "Poe," he smiled as he spoke, making her name melodic.

"Dex," she sang back.

"Why are we here?" He tried to get her back on task.

"To buy a dresser. Obviously."

He shook his head. "Because."

"Because you broke it?" Her brow cocked up as she stood, abandoning her pursuit of opening each and every drawer in the store, and looked at him.

"Why did I break it, Poe?"

The open look of her eyes temporarily closed, and his heart lurched. He hated that guarded look. Hated that she thought she had to hide anything from him. "Well, you see..."

Dex leaned in, desperate for her answer.

"I was just a little worried that I would bite you when I orgasmed and devour your soul." She pinched her fingers together, holding her hand in front of her narrowed eye. "Just a smidge worried."

Likely more than a smidge if the state of her dresser was anything to say about it.

His lips pursed in thought. His mind went through all his immortal knowledge, trying to figure out just what soul-devouring being Poe could be. A soul was a celestial thing, it couldn't be handled by just any being. Very few immortals... if any. Souls were kind of above their magic.

Casters could mark souls, curse them, but devour? He couldn't think of a being who could.

"Poe, what are you?" he asked, unable to swallow the question down. What she was didn't matter, not to him, but it mattered enough to keep them from the thralls of the passion he was so desperate to get back to. So much of her body he hadn't explored, putting it off like a fool, thinking they had the entire night — and day — ahead of them to discover every nook and cranny of one another.

Her chest inflated with kept breath as she pulled her bottom lip with her teeth. "I'm a bit of an oddity, I guess. Succubus mother, which is all well and good." Poe wagged her brows at him and he stifled a laugh. She really was absolutely adorable. "On its own, I supposed I would have been happy with that. Command of a dreamscape. Those badass wings and horns you could hold on to while I suck you within an inch of your life." She sucked air through her teeth. "Its too bad my succubus mother decided she wanted a different kind of strange and set her sights on a reaper."

"What?" He couldn't keep in the outburst. Mating with a reaper was unheard of. They were neutral beings who often didn't bother themselves with the affairs of mortals or immortals alike. It made him wonder just how much of a force Poe's mother was to steal one's attention. To capture one's stony heart in her hands and make it hers, carve her name in it with her pointed nail. It was impressive.

As impressive as he had no doubt Poe was.

She blew her bangs up off her brow. The curls were as stubborn as she was. They lifted and fell right back into their place. "Do you ever wonder why more immortals don't have offspring with beings outside their species — their realms?"

Dex had never thought much about it. He was an outcast even where immortals were concerned, which meant he rarely socialized. He spoke about the affairs of immortals even less, the few friends he kept as mortal as he was once.

"No," he answered.

"Because magic is unpredictable. It does what it wants. Follows no path." Poe's eyes intensified, flashing scarlet while silver swallowed up the line of her pupil. With a roll of her eyes, she turned and continued her perusal of the drawers. "Or so they say."

"So they say," Dex repeated.

"I guess they're right. I mean... I'm pretty unpredictable. I have a succubi's hunger for lust, unfortunately it can't be satisfied unless I top it off with the taste of death. The cherry on top. Magic, magic, magic. So unpredictable." She huffed, moving to stand in front of a six drawer black dresser that was two drawers wide and three drawers down. "Instead of delivering souls to Death like all the other reapers, I devour them." She chuckled under her breath. "Silly magic."

Devour them.

Poe devoured souls. That should bother him more than it did. Should shake his foundations as he looked at the beautiful woman in nothing but an oversized t-shirt, bike shorts, and trainers. The shirt's neck hole was too big, making one of her shoulders tease him with her delicious brown skin. She gestured to the dresser. "This one."

He nodded, uncaring of the dresser. "So when you kicked me off..."

"You awake a hunger in me far more intense than any I've ever had before. A lust so heavy, I sink into it and am unsure if I'll be able to climb my way out. My only hope is to keep sinking and hope I come out the other side. One bite wouldn't be enough, which is funny, because I know it would be a bite too much." Her words held a graveness to them, but that smile was in place. Slightly unhinged. A tad too wide, too perfect. Eerie and beautiful. "So I kicked you."

His heart seized in his chest, lifted up in his throat under the fluttering wings of those damned butterflies. It was a sensation he wasn't used to. One that hadn't afflicted him since he was alive. It felt so constant lately. Made him feel sick to a stomach that didn't feel sick anymore.

"You were protecting me." He was trying to understand her. He needed to understand this woman. It only made sense, since he was already lost to her. "When you kicked me... and every day, when you keep your distance, taking your little photos."

"It's a curious thing... loving something so much, you leave it where it is. Just let it be. Knowing you're a storm it will never survive. Vicious and wild. I loved you that much." Her finger traced the edge of the dresser as she spoke.

Suddenly they were no longer in IKEA surrounded by furniture. It was just the two of them in a world all their own.
A world where Time removed himself from the equation and
each breath held a lifetime in it. Dex stepped up behind her, the
expanse of his chest against her back making her seem small,
though he knew she was anything but a vulnerable thing, even
like this.

"Loved?" Dex dipped his head and whispered into her ear
as his hand rubbed across her lower belly, holding her against
him. "Do you love me no longer?"

"Only a little more than yesterday... a bit less than tomorrow."

That answer fed a hunger in him that didn't exist until yesterday. "As someone who loves me, you should know I require
a love a lot more selfish than the kind you've offered me so far.
Something so demanding, it makes me wonder just how much
of myself I'll have to carve off to give to you to keep you satisfied.
Something that makes me ache as it destroys me."

"Painful pleasure." Poe chuckled as she shook her head. "If
only you knew just what I'd offer you. You would deny me
before I even finished describing the kind of destruction I could
bring."

Dex dragged the side of his face against hers, knowing the
ache his stubble caused in her flesh. It was the only taste he
could give her there surrounded by mortals and furniture. A
whisper of the pain that would come later. "It's funny. All those

pictures and you failed to capture that I would deny you nothing."

"I'll devour your soul," Poe warned, her head falling back on his chest. Her eyes bore up into his, making him wish she'd do just that.

"You can try," he grinned. She truly had no idea.

"I'm a monster, Dex. Ravenous and unforgiving. Any love I have to offer is as tormented as I am. Depraved and final. You won't survive me."

"We're both monsters... and I've survived far worse."

"Nope." Poe pried at his fingers and tried to release herself from his hold. "I can't. I've kept you too long. Loved you too long."

"Have you really loved me if it wasn't a love I wanted? This sweet, treasured love isn't the kind of monsters, and haven't we both admitted to being just that?" He tightened his hold, keeping her against him. "Love me, Poe. Destroy me. Devour me if you need to."

"Your soul," she tried to reason.

If only she knew.

All this time was a wasted thing. Both of them so foolish. She denied him all she had to offer because her bite was one of death, unknowing of how he'd already slumbered in Death's embraced. Laid with him. Rested in his arms until he was a husk of who he once was, only to be released. Rejected. Reborn.

Her father's magic, no matter how twisted and unpredictable housed in the beauteous body he held against him now, had no power here. Not with him. Her mother's magic — that was something he craved now. A desperate need pushed a groan up his throat. He pressed it against her brow with a kiss.

"My soul was denied by Death himself a long time ago. Do you fancy yourself stronger than Death?"

Poe whirled in his arms, chest pressed against his as she looked up at him. That little knot he wanted to drag his tongue over appeared between her brow as she frowned. "What?"

"You can't devour my soul, Poe. It's cursed. To be abandoned by Death until this body wastes away to nothing... and that isn't a common thing for an immortal. You'd only provide me a pain I'd enjoy, beautiful monster."

"No," she argued. "Dex, you—"

"I'm a zombie."

9

A ZOMBIE!

Her mouth fell open, the words escaping her.

Zombies were about as rare as she was. Undead. Cannibals. Apparently, extremely sexy with an ass she could bounce a toonie off of. She'd heard about zombies, of course she had, growing up with a reaper as a father. They were punished. Cursed souls forbidden from ever being delivered to Death. Destined to live out an immortal life living off flesh, until their bodies withered away to nothing, turned to dust, their souls finally free from the flesh of their undead body.

In all her life, in all the realms, she'd never met one.

She'd heard whispers, everyone had. Well, most immortals that hung around crowds like reapers, necromancers, clairvoyants, and the likes. As someone who was an outcast amongst her mother's people, and equally cast out amongst her father's, Poe liked to dance around people who almost fit but didn't.

The ones who told stories of zombies in hushed whispers while watching her warily from the corner of their eyes.

Beings who always made her long to meet one. Something as tortured as she was sure she was. Stories of beings who seemed more like legends. A story always told but never something seen.

Dex.

Dex was a zombie.

She stood with that information bouncing around in her mind before she pulled her phone out of her pocket, snapped a photo of the location tag attached to the side of the dresser, wiggled out of his arms, and walked away.

"Poe?" He quickly fell into step behind her. "Don't you want to talk about this?"

"No."

An exasperated breath left him, but he kept pace with her. "I know it's likely unexpected. We're not exactly an abundant being. Most people mistake us with the undead, temporarily re-animated bodies usually attached to marionette strings pulled by a necromancer, but there are so few true zombies in existence. In any realm. You likely didn't think you were following a zombie around Toronto, which I get, but this can be a good thing. A great thing, even. If we could just talk—"

"No." She had absolutely no interest in talking. They'd wasted enough time already.

Dex stopped in his tracks.

Poe stopped too. She turned to see him standing there, hands in his pockets, looking destitute. And hell, if that wasn't a good look on him too. There was something so beautiful about the broken. So resplendent in the tormented. A darkness most would fear, but she wanted to frame. Hang on her walls. She supposed that's why she had so many photos of Dex.

That, and because he was hers. He had been from the first moment she set eyes on him. From the moment she scented death and despondency on him like a cologne she wanted to roll around in. A pheromone meant just for her.

And it worked wonders.

Closing the space between them, she took his hand and jerked him after her. "Hurry up," she demanded.

"What?"

"You're stopping. Just standing there like a sexy statue, like we don't have somewhere to be." She rolled her eyes at his adorable idiocy. She didn't want to spend all day in IKEA.

"But, I—" he cleared his throat. "I'm confused."

"I know... and it looks good on you." Poe grinned at him over her shoulder. She made her way to the stairs and practically hurled herself down them to get to the bottom. It was a good thing Dex had a firm grip on her hand. He was likely the only thing keeping her on her feet.

She'd be so much more graceful with wings, she thought. Or if she could just float ominously around. Oh well. She couldn't do a thing about that now.

She cut through the marketplace area to the warehouse where she knew her selected dresser waited to be loaded onto the un-steerable cart and brought to her truck. She hurried through the task, a clamouring Dex close behind her. It wasn't until they were wheeling the dresser out to her truck he tried again.

"Poe."

It was cute seeing him like that. That cocky air covered in a vulnerability that made him all the more scrumptious to her. Like he needed her. How she desperately wanted to be needed by him.

"Mhmm." She pulled open the hatch of her truck, loading the two boxes that would make up her dresser.

Dex scrambled to help, though she didn't need it. She could easily get these into the bed of the truck on her own. She supposed it would be weird to anyone watching to see her lift these boxes all by herself. Sometimes she forgot she had to at least try to *appear* mortal. She rolled her eyes at the effort it took.

"Are we... *good?*" Dex asked.

She closed the tailgate and leaned her arm on it, a smile on her face. "Yeah. Why do you ask?"

He shoved his hands in his pockets, lifting onto his toes before he dropped back down. "Oh, I don't know. Maybe because I told you I'm a..." He dropped his voice to a whisper as his eyes looked over the countless mortals moving around the parking lot. "*Zombie*, and then you went from relaxing and taking your time to rushing around."

"Ah." She nodded slowly with realization. "And you think it's because I'm trying to get away from you?" What a silly man.

"Yes. I mean... I say zombie and then you're all—"

"In a rush," she finished for him.

"Yes. So?" His shoulders lifted.

"So?" Did he always have that pale blue around his pupil, a little cloudy? They were beautiful. Captivating. And those lips. The slight purse there as he waited for her answer.

"What's going on, Poe?"

"Oh. Now that I know I can't kill you, I fully intend to ride you as close to death as I can manage. Kind of immediately. Hence, the rush."

Dex's eyes widened slightly at her admission. "You're hurrying so we can have sex?" His words were slow, spaced out with his confusion.

"Yeah. I mean, you have to build my dresser first, since you broke it. But right after that, sex. So much sex." Poe wagged her brow and reached for the cart.

Dex's hands closed over the handle first. "Let me."

Poe chuckled to herself as she watched him cross the parking lot to return the cart, excitement in his step. She turned to round the side of the truck and pain erupted in her brow. Her hand came up, blood dampening her fingers. "Ouch. What the fuck?"

Her eyes lifted and met the hard gaze of a man. He stood in front of her with a scowl on his face, a gun in his hand. He moved to bring it down against her brow again, but she caught his wrist, squeezing it painfully.

"Stop that," she chided.

"Why are you so strong?" he hissed between his teeth before the gun dropped from his grasp.

Poe gave a quick look around the parking lot, forcing a smile as she backed him into the side of her truck. Her eyes caught on a woman who watched them, eyes suspicious. "Babe," she dragged the word out with a breathy giggle. Her hands planted forcefully on his chest as she leaned into him and sunk her teeth into his neck.

He tensed for a second, before he went limp in her arms.

She watched the woman wander away, satisfied with the act she put on. Likely annoyed with their public display. Aggravation kept her from feeling the satisfaction the taste of death usually gave her. Great, now she had a body she had to get rid of. And it hadn't done anything to curb the tight coil in her stomach, the one that had been compressing over the past few days.

"What is with the assholes lately?" Poe huffed, noting there were too many people to shove this guy in the back of her truck. Opening the driver's side, she shoved him over the bench seat and settled him in the middle. She reached across, fastening the seatbelt over his shoulder.

Hands wrapped around her waist, tensing on her belly as Dex looked over her shoulder. "What's this?"

Poe turned in his arms and watched as dark veins travelled under the skin from the sides of his face. His nostrils flared as his fingers brushed along her temple. The wound healed with her feed, but she knew the blood was still there. "Oh, you know. Just making friends."

"He hurt you?"

Her hands cupped the sides of his face as his eyes turned milky and bloodshot. "Dexy. You have to calm down just a tad. At least until we're in the truck driving the body away from the scene of the crime."

A kiss was pressed to her temple. He held her bangs from her face, his tongue swiped over her flesh to clean the blood from her brow. Dex shuddered, his body tensed as the muscles in his jaw jerked. It sent a shiver down her spine as he lifted her into the truck. "Let's go."

Poe sat on the edge of her bed, stark naked as she watched Dex put together her dresser. She had to pull her truck into the garage when they got back to her house. Dex was nervous about someone stumbling on the body she moved to the back — like she didn't do this all the time.

Like she wasn't a pro.

Such a small thing to keep him happy.

She liked watching him in her space. He belonged there. On her floor with all her tools around him. Busy building her dresser. A look of concentration on his face, a crease between his brow. She knew mortal women found stuff like this attractive. Like a display of his manliness. She would much rather see him as he was in the parking lot, inhaling the scent of death on her and angry she'd been damaged before she devoured a soul.

Possessive.

Dark.

Magnificent.

She clenched her thighs together, the need for friction almost unbearable. She needed to scratch this itch. Her succubus blood had gone too long without being appeased. It burned through her veins, making her ache.

Dex hustled her into the room, stripped her down, cleaned her brow and set her in the place she currently sat. Told her not to move.

So here she sat. Loving the command in his voice when he demanded she stay where he could see her.

"You know..." Poe started. "If you would let me out of your sight for just a little while, I could get rid of the body and we could meet up here and finish what we started." She wagged her brows at him, her underlying meaning obvious.

"No." He effortlessly picked up the black frame of the dresser and set it where the pieces had been before he cleaned them away. He stood back, hands on his hips as he looked it over. Satisfied, he picked up the drawers he'd assembled. "I don't want you out of my sight. That guy attacked you in broad daylight. In a crowded parking lot. Plus..." He set the drawers in the frame and began arranging the decor — whatever was still in one piece —back on top. He turned slowly, looking her over.

That adorable, unsure look returned to his face.

"Plus..." he started again. "There's no point in you burying the body when I'll only follow you and dig it back up."

Her brow cocked. "You're the one who dug them up?"

"You knew they were dug up?"

Poe waved her hand, dismissing the question. "Well, the last guy who attacked me forced me to bring him to the bodies and boy... was he mad when he realized they weren't there. Confused the hell out of me too. Especially when he kept barking *Are you fucking with me?'* trying to be all intimidating." She shook her head at the silly thought that she would be intimidated, even for a moment. "Mortals are so funny. He just kept waving his gun around, shooting me." She scoffed at the memory. "Ridiculous."

Those black veins appeared beneath his warm brown skin as it darkened. His hands wrapped into fists at his sides. "Someone else attacked you? Because of the two bodies from the last few nights."

"They must have been really important, or something. All this fuss..." she sighed and lifted her shoulders. "Oh well. So, you've just been digging them up. Eating them."

Dex cleared his throat. "Yeah. Um. I... don't usually get to eat flesh that fresh." With his part-time job in the morgue, he could often get away with a missing arm or leg here or there. Mostly, he had to be happy for the organs no one would miss.

"So..." Poe got to her feet and closed the space between them. "So, you need me?" She pressed her palms against his chest, let them run over him, felt the chill of him she loved more than she ever had any heat.

His hand lifted, cupping around the back of her neck. "Yes."

"Is that why you're here?" She was a little afraid of his answer. She wanted him to be there because there was a pull deep in his chest that forbade him from being anywhere else. Something that grew tighter with space between them, that made each breath a hollow thing that burnt their lungs. She wanted the darkness in his chest to seep into hers until they both danced in that darkness together to music only they could hear. Screams of death and whispers of something obscure and delicious.

"No."

"Are you so sure?" *Please, please let him be sure.* She held her breath as she waited, standing on her toes, her eyes moving back and forth between his.

"You haunt me, Poe. My heart was a decaying ball of flesh and nothingness until I set eyes on you. You started its beating — as much as I wish you didn't. It beats for you, and I worry what will happen when you're not around to keep its rhythm."

As if she would ever let him go now. "You were haunted long before me, Dex. I can see it. I can see the way you're full of nothing but demons you refuse to silence just as much as you refuse to feed them."

The corner of his mouth turned up in a sad smile. "I'm just flesh wrapped over the demons I deserve."

"Aren't we all?" Poe's brow quirked up, understanding in her eyes. She knew what it was like to be endlessly tormented. To be afflicted by the very makeup of who she was until all she could do was succumb to it. Let it fracture her mind enough that the madness that slipped in found happiness. Her demons were content — and in time, she'd make sure his were too.

"No. Not like me. Not like this."

A pout touched her lips as she clasped her hands on his face. "Aw, my undead prince. You're adorable. This plight you feel so plagued by, it's not the curse you make it out to be. There is something so beautiful in a sorrow deep planted. In the cracks it makes in your soul to tether itself in the depths of you. In the demons that find home in the obscurity your sins paint beneath your flesh. They transform us, don't you feel it? Don't you feel how different you are from what and who you were before?"

Her life before she accepted who and what she was had been constantly clouded by sadness. Now, she knew joy.

Lifting a hand, she ran her finger along the crease between his brow, trying to soothe it. Erase it. "You're a masterpiece of woe."

Dex chuckled. "I can't say anyone's ever called me that before, or anything remotely similar."

She pressed a gentle kiss to the tip of his nose and revelled in the way it made him smile. "Hmm, all that tells me is you've kept poor company with people who never really look at you."

His hands wrapped around her waist. He lifted her from the floor until her legs wrapped around him. She held onto him, her hands around his neck. "You're trying to distract me."

Poe pressed her lips against his. The taste of him made her feel dizzy, fed the parts of her that longed for death. He breathed it into her, stirring her stomach. "From what?" she broke the kiss long enough to ask the question, but couldn't deny herself another taste. Another capture of his chilled lips.

Dex groaned, breaking the kiss to stare into her eyes. "From the two men who attacked you. I won't let it go, Poe."

Back arched, Poe pressed her breasts into him. "But they're dead." She needed to persuade him to drop that for now. To forget about the stupid men who kept popping up in her life, forget about how she'd get rid of one and another took their place. It was tedious, but she could hold her own. She was strong — and hungry.

"Poe," there was a warning in his tone, but a wiggle of her hips and a kiss to his neck made him groan again.

She could wear him down, she knew she could. Pesky mortals were low on her list of things to worry about. If they wanted her so bad, they could try to come for her. They'd end up just like Adam and Fiona — and whoever the man was in her truck. She wasn't worried.

He caught her wrist as her hand slipped in the waistband of his pants. "Poe."

"Listen. Sex first, worrying about whoever is after me second. Deal?" She needed him. Her succubus blood was going to combust inside her if he made her wait any longer. "Sex first. Please," she whined.

"Fucking hell."

10

PEX

H E WAS BEWITCHED. ENCHANTED by the very sound of her voice. It went inside his ears like a toxin that made his flesh vibrate and need overcome him, so different from the one he was used to. This hunger wasn't for flesh and blood — it was a thousand times more dangerous.

Poe was all he wanted. The sound of his name from her lips, the whine in her throat, he was helpless to deny her.

They flew across the room, his weight pressed into hers as he sunk his head into her neck and inhaled her. His tongue lapped at her flesh, tasted her sweetness tinged with the tiniest bit of salt. The spice beneath it all was calming and enticing at the same time. Like blissful sleep. It filled his senses, overloaded them, until his hand snuck between them and his fingers ran through the dampness at her core.

Surges of lust assaulted him. Wave after wave that made him a desperate thing that needed to feel her. On his hands, in his mouth, on his cock. It was overwhelming, something he'd never felt before. His mouth watered, but not in anticipation of eating her flesh. It was something else. Something deeper.

He wanted to bite her. To sink his teeth into her skin, but for a different reason entirely. He wanted to mark her. Make her his.

It confused him.

"I don't understand this," he whispered the confession against her skin. "I don't understand how I've craved nothing but flesh for almost a century. Tormented by the way it feels to rip it from someone's bones, only to suddenly feel I would give it all up, starve myself until I was a husk of nothingness if it meant I could have you instead." His hips rolled as the thickness of him rubbed against the inside of his jeans. His soiled boxers were abandoned when he got dressed to replace her dresser.

Poe's hand wrapped around his own. She controlled his hand as she pushed his fingers into her core. He felt her clench around his fingers, hold them tight as she moved his wrist and her hips to ride them. "Why not have both?"

"Both?" He couldn't find sense in her words.

"Fuck me, and then take a bite out of me."

She said it like he wasn't this flesh hungry thing. Like he wouldn't take a bite too much and regret the consequences.

"I don't fear your bite, Dex. I've survived much worse." Her body shuddered, her pussy tight around his fingers. She yanked his hand free and sat up, shoving him down onto the floor. "Shall we give you a reason to bite me, Dex?"

He chuckled, "Like what?"

Poe shoved him onto his stomach and pulled his hands toward the legs of her bed. "Don't move."

Dex obliged her. Partly because of his curiosity and partly because the lust inside him was too much to think through. How mortals survived the touch of a succubus was beyond him. He felt like he could barely breathe through it.

Leather straps wrapped around his wrist before they looped around the leg of her bed and she secured them around the other. It looked like any other leather, until he tugged against it and the vampiric script scrolled across it, dripped in blood before it vanished when he relaxed. These weren't restraints he could get out of, not even with his strength. Vampires had the best bondage equipment. "Should I ask where you got these?"

"Don't tell me you haven't been to any of the hives on orgy night. What kind of immortal are you?" She disappeared from sight. Her hand swatted his ass hard before he heard her rummaging.

Vampires were sexual beings. The thought of frequenting one of their many orgy nights had been one that crossed his mind, but he couldn't trust himself not to lose control. As immortal as vampires were, if he ripped their throat out, they'd die just like everyone else.

Cool steel pressed against his lower back and he looked over his shoulder to see the shine of a blade. She grinned at him, eyes wild, as she cut through the back of his slacks, slowly. He felt the tease of the blade against the flesh of his ass as she cut down the centre of his pants at the back. When she was satisfied, she shoved the cut fabric down his thighs.

The palms of her hands caressed his ass, so slowly and so lightly it made him shudder. He pulled at the restraints and watched the script appear again, only to disappear just as quickly.

Her hands left him and something cool smeared over his ass. Her fingers rubbed it between his cheeks before they teased his hole.

Fuck, she wasn't going to shove something inside him, was she?

Dex groaned.

"You seemed to take wood in your ass like a champ earlier," Poe teased. Her fingers slowly worked into him while her opposite hand wrapped around his cock and slowly pumped.

"Fuck," he hissed.

His head fell between his shoulders and he pressed his brow on the floor. Pleasure made his cock throb. Her hands hit all the right spots, pressed all the buttons. The warmth of her hand was enough to make his knees shake on the hardwood as he wondered how much of that was just her body heat and how much was her magic.

"Let's see just how much you can take, ghoulie."

"Ghoulie?"

"What? You don't like it?"

He'd like anything she called him, but it had been unexpected. Her fingers curled before he could say anything, making him groan. The sound vibrated through his chest as he tried to breathe through a sensation that was quickly becoming unbearable. He wouldn't last, not like this.

Her hand slapped off his ass, and she pulled her fingers free.

The absence of her fingers in him left him feeling empty. As unbearable as it felt being so thoroughly worked, he nearly whined at the absence of it.

"A moment of honesty, ghoulie. Have you ever let anyone sink into you before?" Her fingers moved between his cheeks, teased him, made him want to back up into her and take her fingers again.

Had he?

"Nothing more than a plug," he admitted. "And that was a lifetime ago." Sex was a craving he didn't have often. When he did, he appeased it quickly. Usually without fuss or fun.

"Well, that's about to change," she purred. Something pressed at his entrance, and his body relaxed, excited for the ride he knew she was about to take him on. "Here's what's going to happen. I'm going to fuck you. I'm going to make your toes curl and your cock leak and even when you beg, I'm not gonna to let you come."

"Fuck," he hissed. He looked back over his shoulder at her on her knees behind him. She wore a leather strap on that secured around each of her legs and her hips. The dildo in it was black at the base. Etched in the same way a hoof would be, but the length of it was red and ribbed with a bulbous head.

"This is apparently what mortals think a demon cock looks like." Poe ran her hand up and down the length of it set between her legs, her back slightly arched as she spread lube over it. "I've fucked a demon or two and you know what... it's actually pretty close."

Poe pushed the head slowly into him. The pressure stole away any rebuttal he may have had. His hands wrapped in the straps around his wrist, tugged at them as he held his breath and took the thick length in.

"Breathe," she cooed.

He did. He took slow, even breaths as he was filled with the thick length of her strap on.

"Let me help." Her hand rested on his ass, and wave after wave of pleasure moved through her palm. It was hot. It was brilliant. It made his cock leak and his heart race. Fogged his mind and tightened his throat. His eyes rolled back in his head on a groan.

"Poe," he moaned.

She was slow. She took her time as she inched into him. Her hand wrapped around his waist and took his cock in her hand. Her palm slicked with lube as she jerked him.

He'd never had sex with a succubus before, but as she slowly filled his ass and worked his cock, he saw what all the excitement was about. Each movement was precise, meant to draw out every inch of his pleasure.

Against her instruction, he held his breath. Hoped without breath, he could stay here. Standing on the precipice of his pleasure.

Dex didn't breathe again until her thighs hit the back of his. She wiggled her hips, not quite a thrust, but a movement that pressed something inside him that made him groan and his eyes fall closed. "Poe," he hissed through his teeth.

"Yes, ghoulie?"

"With these straps, I'm surprised you went with a mortal dildo." It wasn't what he wanted to say. What he wanted was to beg her to fuck him until he forgot who and what he was. To work his cock in her hands until he came all over her floors. Drive his knees into the floor and make him ache.

Poe lied over his back. He felt his shirt cut away before her bare breasts pressed into him. "I have no need for magic here, ghoulie. Or can you not feel that already?"

He did. Wave after wave of pleasure pulsed through his veins, made him feel more alive than he'd ever been. "Will you bite me?"

She slowly pulled out of him, and he groaned. "If you're bad."

"I thought rewards come when you're good."

The head of the dildo almost left him, but she thrust forward slowly. "Not for monsters."

He tugged again, and his restraints tightened. "How can I be bad?" he asked. He wanted the instruction hoping it would end with permission.

Poe slightly quickened her pace and his toes curled. "Aren't you bad already?"

Fuck, he was. Dex was so bad, he knew that. He was unbridled sin, cursed for the life he lived as a mortal man. He was wretched darkness that crawled into something pristine and sullied it with his very presence. There was no forgiveness for him. Dex was as bad as they came.

"Yes," he groaned.

She lifted her weight off his back and for the first time in he didn't know how long, he felt cold. He wanted the heat of her skin searing into him. Her hands wrapped around his hips and she pulled him back to meet her. The sound of skin against skin rang through her bedroom, broken up only by his ragged breath.

"Poe," her name was a warning. He was going to come. He couldn't hold out much longer.

"No. You haven't earned it." Her hand rubbed over the head of his cock and collected his precum. It dripped out of him with an abundancy he'd never seen before. Contant. It puddled on the floor between his knees. She used it to rub over him. "Bite me."

Panic moved through him, but it was brief. She hit something inside him that made him see stars before she pulled out, just the head of the dildo seated inside him. "I can't."

"You can," she argued lightly. "And you will, if you want to come."

His groan was desperate as he dropped his brow back to the floor. "Poe." Biting her could kill her, especially like this. Especially when he already felt so out of control.

"Bite me," she repeated lightly, thrusting into him.

"Fuck," he hissed.

"Bite me, ghoulie, and I'll let you come." Her grip wrapped around his thigh and she flipped him easily on his back. His cock bobbed against his stomach as her thighs rested on the bottom of his ass, a smile on her face. She rolled her hips and his bottom lip went between his teeth. "Bite me," she demanded, voice more firm.

With her body laid over his, she rolled her hips again and licked a line down his throat.

This was a different kind of sex. He'd taken. Sated. Used. This was giving. This was surrendering and accepting a pleasure unlike any that had ever been held out to him. The tips of her teeth lightly pressed into his throat.

Dex groaned. "Yes."

"We'll have to trust one another then. A bite for a bite."

He shouldn't. "Yes."

"You first." She thrust again.

Her lips ghosted against his, the briefest of kisses, a tease of a taste. His thighs clenched around her hips, his feet planted on the floor as she offered her neck to him. Everything in him told him not to. To be careful with her. His mouth opened, lips against her skin.

"Bite me."

Another thrust of her hips and he sunk his teeth into her. His eyes rolled back as her blood flooded his mouth. Everything in him tensed and shuddered. His ass tightened around the dildo as cum spurt from him, coating the space between them. His eyes rolled back as his tongue traced the wound he left behind.

This was ecstasy. Paradise. This was as close as he would ever come to a redemption that cleansed a soul as black and marred as his.

Her teeth sunk into him, and a groan left him. His toes curled and more cum left him. Constant. A surge that couldn't be stopped. A guttural sound left him, foreign to his own ears as euphoria wrecked him. Blinding light lit up the space behind his eyes and he felt himself go limp beneath her. This was more than pleasure. This was salvation.

His chest rose and fell in quick succession. Rasped gasps left him as he pulled against the restraints, craving the feel of her. He wanted to wrap her up in his arms. Hold her sealed against him, his cum the glue that would hold them together. Keep him from breaking her hold on him.

Poe dragged the dildo out of him, and he shuddered. A hissed breath left him.

"Fuck," it was almost a whine.

The hold of her teeth on him was a suckle that pulled at something inside him. It was raw pleasure.

He felt himself hard between them. Like all the cum that left him wasn't enough. Like with Poe, it never would be. He wanted her like most wanted air. Desperately and constantly.

"Take these off," he demanded.

She mumbled against his throat.

"Take these off. I want to be inside you."

Her fangs left his throat, and his eyes burned at their absence. "You could be inside me just like this." Poe climbed up him.

"No. Take these off. You've had your fun. Played your game. Tormented me. Now, it's my turn."

A grin touched her lips as she reached up and removed the restraints. Dex's hands immediately dropped to the straps securing the dildo to her, and he unclasped the buckles at the side and pulled it off. His hand wrapped around her waist and he lifted her, switched their positions so her back was against the floor. His stomach slid against hers, his cum slightly chilled between them.

"Now that you're free, whatever will you do with me?" Poe grinned, her smile as mischievous as ever.

Dex dragged a hand across her belly, covered his thumb in cum, and shoved it into her mouth. Her tongue was rough pleasure. Textured in a forbidden way that made his cock bob as it longed for the devilish thing. She wrapped it around his thumb, cleaning every drop of cum from it. Thumb removed, he pressed his body against hers, something so hot in the way their bodies were slicked, in the glide of cum covered flesh. He lined himself up and thrust into her. "I plan to fuck you until you're mine."

11

POE

IGHT FELT MORE LIKE home to her than the day. She felt that was the succubus blood in her veins that called her to a dreamscape she could never access. To a shadowed world where she could reign, if only she could find the key and open the door that would lead her there.

The quiet of her house was too loud.

She stretched out, a frown on her face as her fingers dove under her pillow and she felt something hard and crusted there. Lifting it for inspection, she grinned. She knew dried cum when she saw it.

"Fucking pervert," she muttered, though her belly fluttered with butterflies. "Filthy, wonderful, tempting pervert."

Bare feet on the floor, she looked around her empty room and couldn't keep the frown from forming on her face as she searched for Dex, but found nothing. Her hands reached out, the tips of her fingers traced the bottom of the frames as she made her way out of her room and down the hall. At the top landing, she looked down at the first floor.

The scent of death was heavy. It called to the reaper in her.

Hand wrapped around the guardrail, she made her way downstairs. She didn't question the pull in her chest that led her to the laundry room. She had to get to the garage. That's where the death would be.

The death she'd left in her truck.

Dex had appeased her in more ways that she dared thought imaginable. When she followed him — kept her distance — over the years, she used to imagine the lust they'd create together. Heady and rich, it would sate the needy being inside her. Ignite a passion she knew would threaten to burn them both to ash. What she hadn't expected was for him to give her the taste of death she needed.

She'd never been so completely satisfied.

He was the key she needed to unlock something inside her, freeing both sides of her and making her feel completely whole.

A smirk touched her lips as she pulled open the door. The thought of being so thoroughly explored and satisfied under his hands made her giddy. She regretted waiting so long. She should have taken Dex long before tonight.

The garage was dark when she opened the door. A camping lantern was lit on the far shelf against the wall, casting the far corner behind her truck in an eerie light. The cement under her feet was cold, despite the humid air of the summer night. Her steps were silent as she crossed the garage, keeping close to her truck.

A sickening sound filled the air.

It was unmistakable, Poe had heard it before.

It was the sound of flesh being torn. Of ligaments snapping, blood gushing. There was a gnash of teeth. Gargles. Drips.

Poe rounded the back of the truck and looked down at Dex's hunched body. Flesh was taut over his shoulders, the legs of the man she'd thrown in the bed of her truck earlier that night under the truck, and the rest of him hidden behind Dex's prone form.

Dex's head snapped to the side. The sound of flesh separating filled the quiet, wet and chilling, as he yanked the arm off the body. His head dropped as he ate, the hand hung over his shoulder and within her view.

It was a sight to behold. Something that should be terrifying, but intrigued her.

Inching closer, Poe peered over his shoulder.

He must have been out here a while. The man's chest was cracked opened and emptied. Blood covered Dex's arms up to his elbows, his cheeks stained dark as his teeth ripped into the bicep and tore off a chunk of flesh. Dark veins webbed under his flesh, making the skin around it look dark blue and the warm brown of his flesh look lifeless.

Dex was a predator. Raw. Viceral.

His eyes were covered with a fog, making them look milky and distant.

Poe swallowed hard.

The scent of death was a perfume around him that assaulted her senses. It was brutal and wonderful, making the twisted reaper blood in her veins throb with wanting. "Dex," she whispered low. She needed to see him, wanted to look at him in all his macabre glory.

He whirled at her.

Her feet came out from under her as they collided. He straddled her, bloody hands clasped around her face as the hand was abandoned along with the rest of the body, half under her truck. His grip was bruising as he glared down at her with eyes that didn't see. His mouth opened, and his teeth came down hard on the side of her throat.

Her toes curled.

The pain was blinding. It made her tense before she forced herself to relax in the hold of his jaw. The flesh being ripped from her throat wrestled a squeal from her, as her eyes locked onto his. It was agony wrapped in something oddly alluring.

Rough fingers wrapped around her hair, pulled her head back and bent her neck painfully. His heated breath returned to her throat, and she wondered if he was going to bite her again. If she was going to be surrounded by the scent of reapers that came whenever she danced close to Death, knowing he would never accept her open arms. Never embrace her.

Why did that excite her?

All the broken pieces of her mind made her thoughts a mess. One she didn't have the time to sort through — not even with an immortal life.

Blood rushed from her throat. She felt it stream down her neck and pool behind her head, like a halo of death she knew suited her. The taste of blood filled her throat, and she felt the grin stretch over her lips. It was her favourite taste, one that should forever live on her tongue.

The gossamer lines in his eyes retreated. The film lifted. Dex blinked clarity into his eyes before they dropped to lock onto Poe. Shaking hands released their tight grip, only for him to press one back over the wound.

"Poe," he breathed.

"It's fine," she assured, but her voice was a quiet whisper slightly gargled.

"I..." He took in the state of her. The blood running through his fingers was quick and endless. "I didn't mean to. I thought..."

He was making too big a deal of this, and though she liked the look of confusion in his eyes, she didn't like this. Didn't like the way fear transformed his face from the wicked thing she longed to stare at forever to something else. Something that made the depths of her stomach feel hollow and the backs of her eyes burn.

Her hand wrapped around his pressed over his neck and she smiled. She didn't like the tears that rimmed his eyes and made them shine in the dark. It was like he didn't listen to her at all. Like he hadn't heard her when she told him no reaper would ever come for her. Death would never embrace her. He looked at her like a vulnerable thing he'd broken. Irreparable under the force of his hands.

Most people didn't listen to Poe. They didn't listen to her when she told them if they went home with her, it would be the best, but also the worst night of their lives. That it would be the *last* night of their lives. They didn't listen to her when she told them she wasn't the person they should mess with. The succubi didn't listen to her because she didn't have wings and a dreamscape and reapers didn't listen to her because she couldn't move through the realms as easily as they could. Couldn't deliver souls to Death as was their purpose. Her parents didn't listen to her when she tried to tell them about the sting of belonging to both worlds and neither.

It stung a little to see that look in Dex's eyes and know it meant he might not have listened to her either.

She never lied. She didn't see the point. When she said something, she meant it. Still, no one listened.

"Wait... I can just..." Dex swallowed down the rest of his words, choking on them. "'It's so much blood."

"Dex." She wanted his attention. Wanted him to look at her and see he was listening. "It's fine. I just need to feed and then—"

"I knew this was a mistake," he interrupted. "I told myself I would just wish for you. That I would keep you safe, only touching you in my nightmares. In the back of my mind, I always knew this was a mistake. I knew I would touch you and ruin you."

"I'm not ruined." Why wasn't he listening? "I ruined myself a long time ago to make sure no one else could ever ruin me." Somehow, right now, with this frigid air trapped in her chest as she tried to swallow past a tightness that seized her heart, that didn't feel true.

"This was a mistake," he repeated.

Those words hurt more than his bite did. "Dex, if you would just listen to me, you'd realize this is fine. This isn't the end of the world. It's already healing." She knew it was. Her wound would heal — not as fast as it would after she fed, but faster than any mortal would ever dream possible. She could already feel the slow of her blood. The metallic taste abandoned her mouth, making her desperate for it once more.

His eyes dropped to his hold on her neck, lifting just enough to peek beneath. Concern was still etched on his face, but a sigh of relief left him. "You heal... quickly."

"Don't we all?" She didn't know many immortals that didn't heal significantly faster than mortals. Sure, being in their mortal flesh — for those who had another form — slowed the process some, but compared to the fragile things mortals were, their healing bordered on super.

"Most." His eyes glued to the wound before he lifted his hand completely. The blood slowed to something that didn't make him think she was going to bleed out. Bloodied hands ran over his face as he shook his head. "I could have killed you."

"Just as easily as I could kill you." They both knew that wasn't possible.

"Poe," his voice was a warning, as much as it was filled with sadness.

She pushed him off her so she could sit up. She shoved at the curls in her face as she looked at him, scooting back until her back pressed against the closed garage door. "You didn't listen to me. I don't like not being listened to."

Dex signed. "Poe. We can't..." He huffed in a frustrated breath. "Part of this curse is being unable to stop myself when I feed. It's why I try to only feed somewhere remote. I could so easily lose control. Kill."

"You can't kill me," she told him again, frustration mounting.

On his feet, he looked at the blood on his hands. "I won't... I can't do this. I can't put you at risk, Poe. Not you. Never you."

Her brow dropped. "Dex, one feed and I'll be good as new."

"What if I'd gone for the front of your throat?"

"That would have been uncomfortable," she quipped.

"This is not a joke, Poe. I could have killed you."

Frustration stole her words. No matter how much she spoke, he didn't hear her. His eyes were clear, but his mind was too loud to hear past his own thoughts. To listen. Her mouth opened, but her throat was clogged with emotion. He owed her that much. After all this time, after everything, he should listen to what she had to say.

"You're fine..." He looked her over, as though checking that for himself, untrusting of that statement from her. "So, I should go."

"Go?" Where? It was the middle of the night, and he was covered in blood. *They* were covered in blood. How could he just leave her there, bleeding and needing?

"I'll check on you later." He didn't say anything else. He just turned on his heel and took off into the house. Poe stayed where she was, frozen. Her chest heaved as the burn behind her eyes intensified and she tried to make sense of everything that just happened.

So... he bit her.

Big freaking whoop.

She bit people every night... she had to. He didn't mean to hurt her. The guilt he wore after proved just that. Even if he *had* intended to hurt her, it wouldn't matter. What mattered was that he just sat there, looking through her as he told her what they did, what they were, was a mistake.

Poe stretched out her legs, her bare toes brushing through her blood. She traced lazy lines in the cement. Painting the ground with her bloody toes as her mind went completely blank. She listened to the sound of her front door closing.

A balloon of sadness inflated in her throat, strangling her.

It was too good to be true. Of course it was.

She was poison. Her bite was one full of death.

Deep down, she knew she would never be happy. She couldn't be. She could only be the twisted version of happiness she created. Alone. Unhinged.

The gentle throb at her neck reminded her she had a need to fill. Forcing herself to her feet, she reached out and blindly grabbed at the tailgate, dizziness overcoming her. She blinked hard, swallowed down the tightness of hurt in her throat as she lifted her chin high.

She was fine.

She was Poe. A badass fucking succubi and reaper who could devour a soul whole. And that was exactly what she was going to do. She was going to put on her best pair of killer heels, a dress that made her feel like a conqueror, and she was going to go out into the night. Meet someone, take them home, and devour their pretty little soul.

Dex be damned.

12

DEX

P AIN UNLIKE ANY HE'D ever felt in the whole of his life filled every inch of him. It mixed with his regret, a tonic that was bitter as it filled him, poured down his throat and made a home in his veins. He moved through the night like a haunted thing, the image of Poe under him, blood pouring through his fingers, assaulted him. It filled his stomach with bile and tightened his throat.

That smile on her lips as she looked up at him, so Poe. Like he hadn't just ripped out her throat. Hadn't almost killed her. Deranged and beautiful.

The sight of that smile on her face, her jawline splattered with blood, shouldn't make his stomach clench. Make him throb. It was sick. Vile that the sight of her surrounded by death and destruction was alluring to him.

In his life, there were seldom times he longed for an ear to hear his tormented thoughts. Where he wished there was someone who would offer their shoulder when he felt weary.

Let him lay his head there as he whispered his haunted thoughts to them.

He'd tell them there was nothing in all of existence he wanted more than to have Poe in his arms — safe from him. Before her, he longed for the witch who cursed him to forgive him. To wipe the carvings on his bones clean and let him try again. Let him prove he could do better. *Be* better. Now, he would weather this curse for an eternity if it meant he could walk beside Poe. Lie beside her. Be with her.

He'd never eat again. Wither away to nothing until his body could no longer withstand the curse and his soul was untethered from his undead flesh. Freed but all the better for getting to love her, even if only for a little while.

And yet — he couldn't. The scene tonight was proof of that, wasn't it?

The elevator to his condo chimed, and he stepped out into his penthouse. An eternity cursed by a vengeful witch meant he had a long time to accumulate riches. Plus, he liked to be above it all. Liked to look down at the entirety of the city, like animals in a case. He needed only to reach down and pluck someone out. Devour them until they were nothing but bones.

It made him feel like they were right within his reach, while also making him feel confined. Locked away from them. The city safe so long as he stayed up in his tower.

Dex toed off his shoes and kicked them. They hit the wall before they fell to the floor. His bare feet against the hardwood floors grounded him slightly, but his thoughts still reeled. Tearing the shirt off over his head, he threw it to the floor and continued back through the living room and up the steps. He undid his pants, letting them fall in a heap in the hall as he walked along the catwalk above his living room to the master bedroom. The door was thrown open, and he didn't bother with the lights as he crossed the large room to the ensuite and stepped in.

A slap of his hand against the wall and the room lit. He walked over the dark grey tiles on the floor that looked like stone to the standing shower that took up the entire back wall. It had a large waterfall shower head over the ceiling. Two benches on opposite sides set in the same grey stone as the floors. He opened the glass doors and stepped in, set the water to hot and let it rain over him.

It was too hot, searing his skin. Hands planted on the wall, he dropped his head to his chest and let the water rinse all the blood from him. His eyes glued to the swirls of blood at his feet circling the drain. He wondered how much of this blood was Poe's and how much was the unnamed man he ate before she caught him in the garage.

Her face was frozen in his mind.

She saw him rip the flesh from a severed arm and looked at him with morbid curiosity. Like he was something to be admired, not the monster he was condemned to be. Not the monster she *should* see.

Dex's eyes squeezed shut as he rested his brow on the shower wall.

Their night together had proved she couldn't devour Dex's soul as she had so many others. When he came, it erased the hunger that usually forced him out into the night, made him follow Poe to the cemeteries night after night and dig up the bodies she hid there.

In truth, he hadn't been hungry when he went down to the garage. His plan had been to drive him out, bury him just as she would have. As he stared down at that bastard, knowing he hit her, knowing if the body was ever discovered it may lead the police back to her, the answer was simple. He had to get rid of it. This body, and any other Poe had to feed on. He would get rid of them all to keep her safe.

His anger had made him ravenous. It turned him into the monster who couldn't see past his need to feed.

Poe had entered the garage like a ghost. He hadn't heard her footsteps, hadn't heard her voice call out his name, though he knew she did. Knew that's exactly what she would do when she went out to check on him.

'I'm fine.'

Those were the first words he heard as he pinned her down to the floor. Blood from her own neck spurt up into her face. It cracked at him. Made an ache pulse through his bones, unrivalled by anything he'd ever felt or would ever feel again.

He heard those words as much as he didn't.

Regret made him clutch a hand to his chest at the look on her face as she pleaded with him to listen.

Why didn't he?

He wanted to, but the sight of her bleeding made him irrational. All he could do was look at what he'd done with her and be tossed back in time. Back to all those nights spent in her bedroom, watching her sleep. Knowing his hands would bring her nothing but despair.

They had. He'd become the mindless thing he was cursed to be.

No. This time was different. This time, he'd taken a single bite and the taste of her had coated his throat, cleared his mind. It had brought him back, something that once seemed impossible.

Poe was changing him.

'*I'm fine.*' She seemed fine. Up until he turned and walked away.

"Fuck," he growled under his breath. His hand folded into a fist. He slammed it into the tile over and over until he heard it crack under the force. "Fuck, fuck, fuck."

He'd massively fucked up.

Poe was a whirlwind. She was someone who said what she meant all the time. Sure, she might take a round about route. Sometimes it took him a moment to see just where her thoughts were bringing her, where they'd bring him in turn. The satisfaction he felt when he got on the same page as her. When he saw the light in her eyes at knowing they stood on the same path together.

If she said she was fine, she meant it, and he'd done her a huge disservice by ignoring her. By ignoring everything she had to say after he bit her.

"Fuck." Dex turned off the water that slowly cooked his flesh.

He stood there until the steam drifted up into the fan and the air turned cold. His skin pebbled. The very human reaction to the air made him chuckle. Even as a zombie, he could still get the chills. His laughter was a hollow sound that echoed through the room. He waited until the cold got unbearable — something that never would have happened before her — before he stepped from the shower and out into the room.

The only thing to do was to go back to her. To apologize. To try to fix this somehow.

It had been so long since he had to worry about someone else. To consider how his actions would make someone else feel. Though he played the part of a mortal during the day, he was careful not to create ties. The last thing he wanted was for his hunger to overcome him and the mortals he kept company with to become his meal.

Now, he knew that had somehow changed. That Poe had changed him. That she brought life back to his veins, clarity to his mind. Fed his hunger with something else. With her.

Dex didn't deserve her.

He would be better, though. He would listen. For Poe, he would do anything.

Hell, he'd wear a muzzle if he had to.

13

POE

THE THICK BLACK VELVET choker she wore around her neck matched the vibe she was going for. She felt like a scorned queen, and wanted to give off that energy as she walked into the club in her black pumps, her velvet black mini dress with its thin straps, low back, and the cowl neck that made her small breasts look at least half a size bigger. The velvet shimmered in the low lights. The lotion she'd chosen had a tinge of gold glitter in it that made the warm brown of her skin look tantalizing. Her hair was wild curls about her head, thick gold hoops in her ears.

The underground rave happened every Saturday night. Poe knew it would be the perfect place, just out of the city in the slew of warehouses along Lakeshore. She could feel the bass with every step she took toward the building from outside, and it made her smile. Her keys were the only thing she had on her. She had no use for anything else.

Her phone was large. They spent all that time making phones smaller and smaller in the 2000s, only to decide to make them bigger and bigger the past few years. She had nowhere to put it in her dress, and she hated carrying a bag. She often lost them. Plus, there was only one person who would call her anyway, and he had no intention of speaking with her.

Fucking asshole.

Her thoughts warred with her emotions. Her life had been so full of Dex for so long. Days spent following behind him, following a pull in her chest that whispered of just how wonderful he would be for her, a whisper she hadn't known how to decipher. Now, she knew just how right he was for her, and that made her hate the way she wanted to lash out at him.

Stupid fucking man.

If he'd just listened they would be in her bed, tangled in her sheets. Instead, she was out. Busy trying to find someone to feed the need that would set her flesh to right and erase the throb that fuelled her anger.

Thrum, thrum, thrum.

Each beat at her neck reminded her how angry she was.

Stupid Dex. With his gorgeous face, chiseled jawline, sexy grin, and dark eyes. And that dick...

No. The last thing she needed right now was to be dickmatized. She needed to heal up and figure out just how she was going to make him grovel. On his knees, with that tongue of his pressed just right. That would be a very good start.

Poe stepped into the warehouse. The humid air hit her immediately as bodies bounced around to the music, hands held up, drinks in hand. It was stifling, and she loved it. That thought stayed with her as she moved through the crowd, bee-lining her way to the bar. She needed a drink — or several. Just something to take the edge off the pain that awakened the lust in her, made her need that itch scratched.

She should scratch it. Should drop to her knees before whoever she chose tonight, let them pound the memory of Dex from her mind and her pussy. That would teach him.

The thought made her frown. The idea of having anyone else between her legs was depressing. Especially when she knew how well he fit there.

No, she'd get her taste of death and heal, then she'd make Dex regret walking out on her. Make him beg for the privilege of sinking between her legs again.

That'll teach him.

Poe elbowed her way up to the makeshift bar and lifted her hand at the bartender. They were edgy looking with half their head shaved, the other half bright purple hair that hung down to their shoulder in waves. White spacers stretched their lobes, and they had neon green eyeshadow on their eyes. "Vodka. Straight."

A nod was all they offered before they walked to the opposite end of the bar. Hopefully to get her drink. She would hate to take her frustration out on them tonight, knowing without knowing in that way only a reaper could, that they didn't deserve it.

Poe sighed.

Life was hard.

Immortal life was harder.

If she were mortal, she would only have to shoulder the burden of who she was for a short while until they buried her down in the dirt. Gave her body back to the earth and her soul back to Life to determine what she would do with it this time around. Instead, she knew there was no end to this. That her life would continue on the way it was for decades, centuries, millennium if someone didn't come along and figure out how to kill her. Finally tear her soul from its casing and set it loose, to be captured by whatever reaper dared cross her father and deliver her.

Poe sighed again.

The shot slid toward her and she gestured for another before she even picked the first up. Brow raised, they poured another and Poe considered. "A glass," she decided finally.

They obliged and poured half a glass of vodka.

Poe grabbed some money from the front of her dress and slid it across the bar. It was likely nowhere near the fifty bucks she paid, but hopefully when she came around the bar later, they'd be quicker to serve her.

A smile stretched across their face, showing Poe teeth that were slightly askew in a way that added character and made their smile all that much more captivating. She liked when things were a little out of place. When things were tinged in the smallest amount of disorder. She felt a connection with things that didn't quite fit the way they were supposed to. A kinship with the unordinary.

Glass to her lips, she let the drink poured down her throat. It burned delightfully and made the wound at her neck pulse.

"Drinking alone?" The voice was rasped brutality made sweet with the lightest dressing of honey. It was a purr from a wildcat that tightened Poe's core. She didn't turn to look at them right away. Instead, she continued to pour the drink down her throat and waited for it to hit her.

There.

Under the scent of expensive perfumes and lotions and the scent of sugary drinks on her breath, was putrid smoke. The scent of stolen sorrow, silenced screams, and collected tears. This was not a good woman. Oddly enough, that made her perfect for Poe.

Brow quirked, her dark eyes took her in.

She was a tall thing, someone who seemed better suited on a runway than here in this makeshift club. Her black halter top left her midsection bare. The skin of her belly was soft and pale, covered in bright tattoos that climbed up her sides and disappeared in the waistband of leather pants sat dangerously low. Her black hair was pulled up into a high ponytail on her head that was straight and long. A curtain of black that lightly matched the colour of this vixen's soul. Her bright blue eyes felt too vibrant. It was as jarring as the deep red on her lips as they turned up at the corners and took Poe in.

Poe tilted her head and threw back the rest of her drink. A light hum sounded from her throat as the vodka did its job and buzzed just loud enough for her to forget the pain and who caused it. "Yep. I don't like to share."

"Is that right?" The woman reached a hand out and cupped her finger under Poe's chin. It was a dominant gesture. One that showed Poe she demanded her attention as she spoke to her. "I love to share."

"Something tells me you aren't talking about drinks." Poe knew exactly what she meant, but a coy attitude often went a little further with the dominance this woman exuded. She wanted to surprise Poe, to intrigue her. To entice her with a taste of something unknown.

It wasn't unknown to her, but this woman didn't know that.

A mischievous look flashed in her eyes as her grin broadened. "I'm not," she confessed easily.

Poe turned her body to face the woman's, a smirk on her lips. "And just what could you mean?"

Brazen, the woman stepped into Poe's space and lightly pushed some of her curls behind her ear. "I could tell you..." She leaned in close until her lips brushed against the ear she'd bared. "Or, I could show you."

"Could you now?" Poe let the question hang open in the end, wanted the woman to fill it.

"Kate," she offered.

What a boring name. She seemed so much more than Kate. Like a Hemlock or a Oleander. Something that hinted the poison that ran beneath her skin. Then again, how many people would walk into the darkness, if they knew just how endless it would be? How toxic? How thorough? She supposed Kate was the name that caught the unsuspecting.

Poe was anything but.

A sadness pulled at her chest that annoyed her as she pushed away from the bar. "Show me then, Kate."

Kate walked beside her, but she wrapped her hand around the back of Poe's neck. Guiding her like a pup through the crowd.

If only Kate knew this pup had a vicious bite.

The house Kate took Poe to was in a gated community that Poe didn't think existed in the GTA. Kate pulled up outside the gate and punched a code into the keypad before the looming iron gates swung open and she drove her car up the long drive.

Poe's eyes wandered over to Kate over the drive. She felt she would look more at home on a motorcycle than behind the wheel. She had that look about her. Mayhem and speed.

Never one to need an invitation, Poe was out of the car as soon as it stopped. She walked up to the front steps and looked up at the French Provincial style mansion and whistled. "This is impressive."

"Everything about me is impressive," Kate boasted. Her arrogance was as attractive as it was offputting. She straddled the line, making it work for her as she walked up beside Poe and wrapped a possessive hand around her arm. "Come on. Let me give you a tour."

The foyer was equally impressive. It mirrored the look of the outside in a way. Glass, frames, and filigree banisters along the stairs that made their way up along the outer walls of the foyer, big enough to be someone's bedroom.

Poe never saw the point in such grandeur. She had met beings with strength that would force any sovereignty to their knees with little effort who called hovels and caves home. Who was she to think she needed a place like this? Who was anyone?

Money was also something she thought meaningless. It made her long for realms where you could trade something far more meaningful. Curses, spells, dreams, even hopes were currency to some. Paper with pictures of dead mortals seemed worthless in comparison.

Her attention was pulled away from the opulent scene when she realized Kate had wandered off. Poe turned, her heels clicking off the white floors as she made her way further into the house to where she knew she'd be. That pull in her chest that whispered of the obscurity beneath Kate's skin told her just where to go.

Kate stood in a kitchen far too large for any private home. Her hands were braced on the island — white like everything else in this house seemed to be — with two glasses of red wine between them. Her fingers rested on the base as she slid it over to Poe with that smirk that hadn't left her face since they'd met.

Poe flashed her one of her own and crossed the room to take the glass. She held it under her nose, inhaling it. Something sharp hit her senses, made her pupils turn to slits.

Interesting.

She looked over the woman who stared at her with newfound curiosity. "Such a big house. What is it that you do?"

"I work for a very reputable family," she told Poe, her eyes glued to hers. She watched her like she was something behind a glass. A prize she'd captured and could observe at her leisure.

"Seems they pay well. I wonder just what you do to get such benefits." Poe swirled the wine in her glass, watched the way Kate stood unmoving, her eyes refusing to look at her drink.

Her tongue traced her bottom lip slowly before she picked up her own glass and rested her hip back on the counter behind her. "You could say I'm a problem solver."

"Just what problems require such rewards when you provide a solution?" Poe lifted the glass to her lips and swallowed the contents down. The taste of drugs hit her tongue, bitter and wonderful. Glass emptied, she ran her tongue — the forked end held together to appear mortal — over her lips and set the glass down between them. "You must be very good at your job."

"Very." Kate took a small sip of her own drink.

Those skills would earn her nothing here. Poe reached a hand back, lifting her foot to remove one heel and then the other before she stood on her bare feet, heels in hand. "Are you trying to solve a problem, Kate?" Poe asked.

"A very interesting one. You see, my boss's daughter went out a few nights ago in search of her boyfriend... a bit of a hound dog, if you ask me, but then again, most men are... and never came home. We sent out someone to look for her, and he never came back either. Missing. *Poof.* Quite the puzzle, wouldn't you say?" Kate's tone was light, but her eyes were hard.

Poe could practically see her counting the moments in her head. Ticking off the seconds until whatever she'd put in Poe's drink rushed through her veins and did whatever she wanted it to do.

Kate was about to be very disappointed.

"And this daughter, is she a problem solver too?" If she was, she wasn't very good at solving whatever problem kept her from her mansion.

"No. She's more like a princess," Kate replied.

"Is this supposed to be her castle? As far as houses go, this is very impressive. If we are going by castle standards though, this is a tad disappointing. Could use some more velvet drapes, some damp stone." Poe had been in a castle or two in her time. This was definitely not one of them.

"For the right people, their castle is wherever they lay their head. Wouldn't you agree?" Kate's smirk slipped.

This night was about to be a lot more fun than Poe realized. She was about to satisfy some of her anger as well as her taste for death. *Wonderful.* "Am I the solution you're looking for, Kate?"

"I think you are."

"*Think*," Poe playfully repeated the word. "If there's one thing I've learned about mortals, it's that their thoughts rarely amount to anything. Even when they're paid well to problem solve."

"Mortals?" Kate's brows dropped, a look of humour on her face as she shook her head. "And what would that make you?"

Poe set her hands behind her back, her heels still clasped in them as she slowly paced the space. Her feet kicked out, making the movement seem slightly unhinged as she set her feet in sloppy lines, and twirled in place every few steps. "It would make me someone unaffected by whatever you put in my drink. I'd have to give your bartending skills a one out of five. The bitterness of whatever it was would have been better in a sugary drink. Zero for effort." Poe gave her a thumbs down and vibrated her tongue between her lips. "I mean, really."

Kate straightened, her relaxed pose forgotten. "What? How did you...?"

"As far as this princess goes, does she have a name?"

Don't say Fiona. Don't say Fiona.

"Fiona Rinaldi."

Well, fuck. Of course, this was about Fiona. All of this trouble wasn't worth the lay. It really wasn't. She could have gotten her rocks off with someone else and not had their goons and baggage follow her around.

Fiona Rinaldi. Apparently, she was some kind of crime princess.

And to think, if Dex hadn't been such a hardhead and listened to her, they could have been on their third or fourth orgasm by now. She could have her thighs wrapped around his ears, tight enough to make him beg for mercy.

Men.

This would do for now.

Kate watched her face for any indication the name meant something to her. In truth, it meant very little. As troublesome as her death was to Poe now, she was no one. Just another mortal whose soul needed to be devoured to free this existence of the torment they brought. Sure, most reapers had to wait until Death claimed them — but not her. Poe could devour a soul without permission.

Normally, the lives she took didn't even make the news. No one reported them missing. Most people were glad they were gone. The heir to a crime family may not make news, but it would definitely make waves.

"Hmm." Poe pursed her lips, enticed by her predicament. "And you think I killed Fiona?"

"I know you were the last one who saw her alive." Kate pulled open a drawer and tossed photos on the counter. She spread the photos out on the counter, revealing photos of her with Fiona in the club. With Adam. "The last one to see them both alive."

Most would lie, Poe knew that. She'd seen it, lived it. But she didn't really see the point. So instead, she blew air through her lips, let them vibrate before she clicked her tongue. "Well, that's true. Adam was... a quick fix, really. He had a big attitude, but that's about it. But, in a pinch, I tend to make things work." Poe shrugged. "Fiona was out of his league. Her looking for him was really the leap toward her downfall. Everyone's fall to ruin begins with a single misstep, wouldn't you say?"

Kate's face hardened. "Where is she?"

Poe thought of the best way to answer that. She chuckled, the sound light and full of mischief. "That's hard to say."

"What do you mean, *it's hard to say?*" Kate stepped forward, her fist slammed against the countertop. "Where the fuck is she?"

"Well." Poe stepped up to the counter, met the challenging look in Kate's eyes with one of her own. She could easily grab her, pull her over the expensive countertop, kicking and screaming, and sink her teeth into her. She should. But a part of her wanted to see what came next. Wanted to know the pain Kate had in store for her. Wanted to feel a pain that didn't hurt as much as the squeeze of her heart Dex left behind. "It would really depend. She could be at a penthouse, he seems like a penthouse kind of person. Or she could be out on the town." Or she could have been crapped out. She wasn't entirely sure about the specifics of a zombie's digestive track.

That thought made her chuckle to herself.

Kate's hands whipped out, a sleek silver gun in her grasp, but Poe had seen enough to know it wasn't normal. It was something else. Something different.

"Where is Fiona Rinaldi?" Kate repeated.

"Hard to say."

Kate fired.

A slight prick hit her chest, and Poe looked down at the silver dart embedded there. Her hand wrapped around it, and she yanked it free. A small bead of blood lifted from the wound before it dripped and left a slow trail down her chest.

"That's a first." Poe laughed. Mortals were resourceful little things. Their weapons were primal and fascinating. Of all the things she'd been warded off with before, a dart was a first. She'd been stabbed, she'd been shot with bullets, pellets, beanbags, and even arrows. A part of her missed swords. That was a skill just collecting dust she didn't think she'd get to use any time soon.

She let the dart fall from her hand and laughed.

Kate fired again.

Poe sighed. "How many of these does that thing fire?" She felt the light tinge of something in her blood. It was the same buzz the alcohol could leave behind if she drank enough. Faint. A whisper of something that should be a shout.

Another shot.

It was a silent weapon. Kate pressed the trigger, and the dart whizzed toward Poe. There was a slight whistle in the air as it parted, something that likely wouldn't be heard by mortal ears, but Poe heard it.

She wished the shots hurt a little more. The tiny pinch did nothing to overshadow the wrenching pain in her heart. A pain she didn't understand.

Three more shots were fired, scattered over her chest as she stood there with a look that was more humorous than annoyed. It was a funny thing, watching the way Kate's face transformed with each shot. Like the determination that fuelled her to bring Poe there was replaced with a confusion being shoved at her by fear.

"What the fuck?" Kate muttered.

The haze thickened in Poe's mind, making her feel how she imagined most people did when they were drunk. It was wonderful. Like soaring and falling all at once. A sigh left Poe as her head fell back and she basked in it.

Pain erupted in her head as her knees gave out under her. Pain rattled her brain again when her head hit the tile.

Lights out for Poe.

The thought was amusing as her vision darkened at the edges. It hadn't been done before, at least not by mortal hands. She could fight it, she felt that in the depths of her. She could fight off the darkness that devoured her sight. That filled her mind. But she didn't want to. Poe wanted to fall into a darkness that she didn't bring. To lose control, even if just for a little bit.

So she let go.

And she plummeted into darkness.

14

DEX

I T SEEMED SUPERNATURAL THE way he could find her. The way he could smell her in the breeze, feel the pull of her in his chest as he moved through a city of millions as though no one else existed. This city was theirs.

He followed the need inside him — the hunger — to Lakeshore and felt the thrum of the base in the warehouse set away from the city. This place practically screamed *Poe*, and as he sat outside, it made him laugh. Even in her anger, she looked for chaos.

Dex stood there and wondered just how he was going to play this. Shroud in darkness, he stood in the bushes that separated the building from the street and watched the countless mortals stumble in and out of a warehouse he knew was packed with them. How easy it would be to take a bite out of one, to hold them against him as he danced with their lifeless body while the people continued to party around them. None the wiser.

Mortals were such feeble things.

Ignorant to anything they didn't want to know. Blind to anything they didn't want to see. Many could even see the blood in his mouth and convince themselves it was a trick of the mind. The lie would be better than looking a little closer. Seeing an uncomfortable truth.

How unlike his Poe. She wanted to see everything. Wanted to open up every casket and see the rotting corpse inside. Reach into the shadows and see if they'd bite one of her fingers off.

He loved that about her.

He loved *her*.

The admission made the ache in his chest intensify. How easily it happened. She sunk her teeth into him long before last night. So long ago, he couldn't remember the day. Couldn't pinpoint the moment when his curiosity about the woman who stalked him through the busy streets of Toronto turned into giddy anticipation as he searched for her. Hoped for her.

Poe was his, and he was in love with her. Body, mind, and twisted soul.

The door opened, and he held his breath captive in his chest. His eyes flew to the woman who strut out, curls wild about her head and curtained over her brow and that body he desperately wanted to get his hands on, carefully wrapped in a little black dress he wanted to tear off her with his teeth.

Fuck, she was gorgeous.

Dex took a single step from the bushes.

Her hand reached back, and she pulled a woman behind her. The woman looked over Poe with assessing eyes, cold and vengeful.

Everything in him tensed as Poe climbed into her car and they peeled out of the makeshift parking lot where dozens of cars were strewn over long, trampled grass and overgrown weeds. Gravel and dirt kicked up behind the tires as he watched her taillights disappear before he hurried over to his own car.

Unease moved through him.

He couldn't be sure, but he felt like this situation was dicey. She'd already been shot by someone who forced her to bring him to the graves she'd dug for Adam and Fiona, a couple she'd fed off in the nights before he was bold enough to step into her life. The man in the parking lot was looking for them too. Dex knew that.

Whoever that couple was, they were important enough to send out a search party. One who knew Poe was the last person to see both alive.

Poe seemed, at times, invincible. He feared now more than ever that wasn't true.

Watching her lie there, with a halo of her own blood, scarlet and beautiful, around her head as the gargle of her blood made the sound of her voice sound like a melancholy ballad, he realized she was flesh and blood. She could be broken. She could bleed. Being repaired was something she could do, but for how long? To what end?

Dex's grip tightened on the wheel. His foot put more weight on the gas as he followed closely behind the car that moved through the night.

An eternity is a long time to wait for a love you know you don't deserve. The kind that reaches into a hollowed chest full of gossamer strings of hate and regret, and pumped his heart in her fist. Uncaring of how is aches. Uncaring of how much sin he wrapped around it. Fingers blackened by the obscurity that clung to it, Poe brought it back to life. Something like that happened once in a lifetime, if it happened at all.

He felt asleep. Up until now, he was dancing in the nightmare both he and Poe enjoyed. Their game of cat and mouse. Their dark obsession with one another. The way a simple kiss from either of them should mean death to the other. It was dressed up shadows, pretty in the treacherous ways it moved. It was a nightmare he'd been content in, one he could have lived in forever, but now the very thought of losing her jarred him from his slumber.

Dex was a monster. He'd always known that. What he'd never considered was he was a monster orchestrated to be hers. To torment her. To make her bleed. To kill for her.

What were curses if not fate's path for monsters that knew nothing else?

What was Death to those who would never meet him, but an adventure?

Poe was ruined by her lineage, Dex was ruined by his sins. And together, they could dance in the chaos they both thrived in. Create a palace of the wreckage that would feel more at home to them than any paradise ever could.

He'd be her monster.

And he'd show anyone who dared do her harm just how insidious he could be.

15

THE SOUND OF HER bones breaking was like a gong placed beside her ear. It chased away the darkness she surrounded herself with, a blanket she found warmth in, and brought back in the world she never really cared for.

A scream vibrated through her throat, tapered off by a groan as the pain took its rightful place under her skin. As close to Death as she would ever be allowed. A taste of what she'd have to endure time and time again, only to be ignored by him.

Her scream dwindled away to maniacal laughter.

Her head fell back, and she looked around the room. It had cement floors, bright walls. Exposed beams went along the ceiling overhead, spiderwebs around the lights set between them. She was in a basement. The basement of a mansion.

Poe's laugh intensified.

This was class. Even the cement on the floor looked like there was a slight sparkle to it. The beams overhead the same white or cream or eggshell or whatever the hell colour they called what they slapped on every surface upstairs. The lights weren't the lonely bulbs that usually swung overhead in basements. They were set in grey metal. Like fancy plates that seemed ridiculous in a mostly unfinished basement.

Poe pulled at her arms. They rattled as the cuffs hit off the legs of the chair. She looked down, saw the legs bolted to the floor, and the tarp laid out beneath it.

Kate stood in front of her with three men at her back. Her foot rested on a car battery and she held jumper cables in her hand. She snapped them a few times, satisfaction on her face. "That has to be some sort of record, wouldn't you say, Brick? Five darts... and she only stayed asleep for twenty minutes."

A bald man with massive tattooed arms crossed over a broad chest scoffed. "She's some sort of freak. I ain't never seen nothing like it before."

The man beside him, hunched over with his hands in his pockets and blond hair swept back, cocked a pierced brow. "I like them a little freaky. Durable is always a good thing."

The third man's brown hair was pulled up in a bun at the top of his head. His light brown skin made the hazel of his eyes pop as he ran a thick hand down his beard and considered her. "She'd better hope she's durable. We want answers to our questions before she passes out."

Poe's eyes dropped to her arm. She could see the lump of her bone under flesh where she was sure it was broken. "I don't seem *super* durable right now."

Kate's eyes narrowed. "Where is Fiona?"

"Dead."

The bald man — Brick — stepped forward, a menacing look on his face. "You'd better hope that's not true."

Her body thrummed with wicked pain. "Oh? Why's that?"

His hand wrapped around the arms of the chair she was tied to. Her ankles cuffed to the front legs, her wrists to the back. The heat of his breath touched her face. It smelt like whiskey and beef jerky. "Because if she's dead, so are you."

"I'm very much alive."

"Yeah, but that's only because we want you alive. We need you alive to figure out where she is. If she's dead, we have no use for you." Brick bared his teeth at her, light brown eyes intense. "So tell me, you little bitch, do we have a use for you?"

Poe laughed. "I could think of a few, but if you're hoping for me to lead you to Fiona, you're shit out of luck."

"You were the last to see her alive," Kate pushed. "We know you left with her."

"Mhmm," Poe agreed. "Sure did. Took her back to my place. Wanted to see if she was any good at eating pussy. She was." Poe winked at Brick. "She did very well."

The second man licked his lips. "Is that right?"

"Keep it in your pants, Jake." Kate rolled her eyes, cursing under her breath. "None of that matters. What happened after?"

"After," she paused to wink at Jake. "When she was all smiley from me gifting her with the best orgasm of her life, I bit her." She lifted her shoulders, as though that was admission enough.

"You... bit her." The third man looked confused.

"Hot," Jake hissed.

"It doesn't matter." Kate shoved Brick aside. "None of this matters. We couldn't give two fucks about Fiona's sex life." She shot Jake a dirty look when he put his fist between his teeth and groaned. "As sexy as some might find it. What we care about is where she is now."

Poe lifted her shoulders. "Couldn't say."

"You said she was dead," Brick argued.

"I did."

"I'm getting sick of this," Kate snapped.

Brick stepped forward with a mallet in hand and what she could only assume were railroad spikes in the other. He placed one in her thigh right above her knee, and a swift whack slammed it through her flesh and the chair beneath her.

It wasn't quite pain. It was burning. Like something seared through her every nerve and made them all fire at once until she was a mess of nothing but constant suffering. She didn't even notice the second hammered into her other leg. The pain had created a buzz the likes of which alcohol could never achieve.

Fed into the dark blood that was supposed to be neutral, but was tainted when touched by the succubus blood that made her long for the dark delights this pain — or any — offered.

Poe sucked in a sharp breath when she was hit with a bucket of frigid water. She gasped, taken by surprise as a satisfied Jake tossed the bucket away. The bucket banged off the floor as it bounced.

Blowing out a breath, she tried to get the water from her face. Her bangs dripped into her eyes, no matter how many times she blinked. "Well, that's going to drive me crazy."

"We're planning on doing a lot more than drive you crazy," Brick growled. He was definitely the muscle in the group. Barrel chest, serious mug, the frown might as well be one of his tattoos the way it was set permanently on his face. The top of his bald head shone under the lights. Looking at him, she knew he almost always meant business.

How boring.

Poe let out a dramatic sigh. "Well, that's good. Since I already know my way to crazy, I rarely need a drive."

Kate pressed the clips against Poe's bare legs.

Her teeth clenched as jolts of electricity moved through her. It tensed every muscle, her jaw so tight she was sure she'd crack her teeth under the pressure. Her fangs lengthened, cut into the tender flesh of the inside of her cheeks and her inner lips.

Relief was all-encompassing when Kate removed the clips. A sigh left her as her whole body collapsed lower in the chair.

"Where is Fiona?" Kate asked.

A small pout touched Poe's lips, as dramatic as everything else about her. "It's a bit sad no one cares about Adam. I mean, was he lousy in bed? Yes. Was he worth all the trouble? Definitely not. But still... you could ask about him. And the other one... the nameless brute with the trigger-happy finger." If she got his name, she didn't remember it.

"No one gives a fuck about Adam," Brick's stern voice filled the silence.

"Where is Fiona?" Kate asked again.

Poe rolled her eyes. Repetition slowly plucked at the threads of her mind. The same question over and over, with her answer being ignored. It was frustrating. She'd given them the answer. Just because it wasn't the one they wanted, didn't mean she'd change it.

Electricity burned through her. It fried the ends of all her nerves as the clips were pressed to the spikes.

It was a different sort of pain. Not quite the burn of fire, but sharper than the slice of a blade or the tear of a bullet. It was similar to magic, in a way. The way it seared through her veins made them threatened to pop. It was cathartic, like finally setting her feet on the front steps of a home she swore she never wanted to see again, but that her heart still yearned for.

When the clips were removed, laughter shook through her.

"This one has a fucking screw loose," the third man said.

"Tate," Kate warned.

"Well, she does. We've got her hooked up to a car battery and she's just laughing about it. Like she doesn't have the sense to be scared."

"Scared?" Poe laughed, her whole body heaved with the movement. "Why would I be scared?" Nothing but measly pieces of metal and bolts kept her in place. She could get out of them easily enough — if she wanted to. Lucky for them, she didn't. She wanted to feel the way she did now, alive under torturous hands.

Hands that didn't belong to Dex.

"Because we're going to kill you," Tate barked.

"Is that right, *Tate*." Poe chuckled. "Tate and Kate. Couple... twins, maybe?" In truth, they didn't look very similar. "Lovers?"

Jake chuckled and quickly hid it behind his hand, a cough took its place when Kate cut him a look.

Tate leaned in, his hands wrapped painfully around her face. Just a little more pressure, a little more nail, and he could slice little half moons into her cheeks. "You do know we're going to kill you, right?"

Poe blew him a kiss. "Promises, promises."

Fresh pain went through her leg. Her eyes dropped from Tate's face to the blade he just impaled in her thigh. "I keep my promises."

Mortals were so funny. So oblivious. Even after all she'd shown Kate thus far, she still thought they'd accomplish something here. With these weak attempts to break something already so shattered, all they'd accomplish was cutting themselves on her sharp edges.

"This is one you won't be able to keep." Poe wished someone — anyone — would listen to her. Hear what she had to say and believe it.

"Says the woman strapped to a chair and about to be hooked up to a car battery," Jake laughed.

"Mhmm. That's exactly who says it. Quite astute of you, Jakey."

He stepped forward, menace in his eyes. "Don't call me that." The cold tone of his voice only made her laugh again. He was cute. She'd have to see if he tasted as good as she thought he would. Spiced and glorious.

"Maybe she has someone she thinks will come and save her. Did you look into her, Kate?" Tate asked as he swept his fingers through his hair.

Brick stood like a sentry behind them, his hard eyes glued to Poe. Prepared for whatever mischief she'd bring.

Or so he thought. Poe found no one was ever quite prepared for her brand of mischief.

Kate brushed her hair back over her shoulder. "Yeah. I looked into her. There was nothing to look into. She just popped up around ten years ago and there's practically nothing on her."

Tate turned, his voice hushed but not quiet enough for Poe's ears to miss. "That's suspicious. Are you sure she doesn't work for one of the other families? If she does and we kill her without knowing for sure, this could start a war."

"If she killed Fiona, then one has already been started," Kate hissed back.

Poe let an exasperated groan vibrate from her throat. "Ugh. Can we get on with the torture already? Do I have someone who can come and save me? Yes. And he'd actually better, if he knows what's good for him, because he's in big trouble with me right now. Should you be terrified of him? Absolutely. He makes the boogeyman look like the toothfairy. He'll rip your throat out with his teeth and drink your blood as the life drains from you. But..." Poe pursed her lips. "I don't really *need* him to save me. But how romantic would that be?" She sighed as longing filled her chest. "Just swooping in here, covered in blood and flesh, with murder in his eyes. Hot as fuck."

"The fuck?" Jake looked between Kate and Tate. "Are you hearing this shit?"

"She's just trying to get in our heads. Don't listen to her. She's avoiding the question." Kate opened and closed the clips, the threat clear.

"I haven't avoided the question. You asked me where Fiona is, I told you she's dead. Fiona is dead. Adam is dead. The beefy guy with the gun is dead. Dead, dead, dead. And gone. There will be no finding them. There's nothing left to find. Ashes to ashes and all that. Dust in the wind." Flesh in Dex's stomach. Tomay-toe, tomah-toe.

"What do you mean, they're gone?" Kate urged.

How tedious this was. "No one survives the night with me. That's kind of my thing." Well, almost no one.

"So... what? You're a serial killer or something?" Tate asked.

"Or something," she sneered.

Kate shook her head. "No. There would be evidence. Something left behind. Where...?" She was grasping at straws. The answer she got wasn't the one she wanted.

"What would be the fun in that?" Poe chided.

Brick stepped forward, his arms dropped from his chest as he pulled the knife out of her leg. "Well, then I guess we have no use for you."

16

H E FOLLOWED THEM TO an upscale gated neighbourhood. Mansions set back from the road, with driveways you had to be buzzed into. Houses of the elite, he knew the neighbourhood and had considered buying himself one of these obnoxious things once upon a time for the privacy alone.

He parked his car down the block. He wouldn't be needing it. If it got towed, it got towed.

On foot, Dex stalked up to the brick wall that surrounded the mansion. He sunk his nails in the mortar and climbed up. He made fast work of the wall and was up and over it before he had time to think about being caught. A part of him wished someone would stumble upon him. He had a vicious anger in him that craved the confrontation.

The fresh anger would take some off the edge of the rage directed at himself.

He was such an idiot.

Dex landed effortlessly on the grass below. His hands sunk into the pocket of his slacks, his sheer black button down rolled at the elbows and thin enough to not feel stifling in the summer heat.

He strut across the lawn like he belonged there. Dex belonged anywhere he wanted to, and he decided he belonged anywhere Poe was. If she was in this house, it was theirs. Damn the deed, damn the silhouettes of what he knew would be large men standing at the ready by the door.

Without rush, he strolled toward them. He could smell the scent of weed and cigars as he got closer. The slight tinge of alcohol on their breaths as they chatted, none the wiser of the monster that stood in the shadows. Dex's hand whipped out as he stepped up behind the first man. His hand wrapped around his throat and his thick, blunt nails sunk into the tender flesh before he tore it free. Heat covered his hand as blood spurt over his fingers.

The man's hands waved in the air before him as he gasped and gargled on his own blood.

The second man reached quickly behind him and pulled his weapon. "What the fuck?" His wide eyes were still full of surprise as he looked at the man he'd just been conversing with bleed out in Dex's hold.

Dex snarled, teeth bared. He knew the blackened veins left gossamer trails over his face, his eyes dead and sinister.

He fired.

Hold firm, Dex moved the body into the path of the bullet. The first shot sunk into the man's chest, the next into his face as Dex moved him in front of his own. He tossed the body at the man with the gun and watched as they both tumbled back onto the gravel driveway.

One hand shoved casually in his pocket, he brought his foot down on the man's wrist, just as he shoved the body off him. Dex lifted the chunk of flesh in his hands to his lips and bit into it. He savoured the taste, let the flesh and blood roll down his throat as he stared at the shock and disgust on the face of the man who struggled to get his hand free, his gun just out of reach.

"Where is the woman who was brought here tonight?" Dex's voice was cold threats and twisted intentions.

The man spat at Dex, eyes blazing. "Fuck you, you fucking psycho."

He pressed more weight into the man's wrist. He pressed and pressed until he heard the first crack. Mortals and their feeble bodies.

A curse hissed between his teeth before he kicked his heels against the gravel.

Dex put the rest of the flesh in his mouth, felt the way the blood squished from it and leaked down his chin as he watched the man who was likely supposed to be muscle to whoever hid away inside. "We have two options here. You can tell me where she is and I will kill you, or you can hold on to your secret and I eat you alive. Which will it be?"

"Are you fucking kidding me?"

Dropped to a squat, Dex replaced his foot with his hand and reached over the man who struggled to free himself from his immovable hold and grabbed onto the dead man's wrist. He pulled him toward him, his body half draped over the man who he knew was just about to tell him what he wanted to know. Lifting the arm to his mouth, he sunk his teeth into it.

He pulled at the flesh like jerky, ripped it free from the man's arm before he chewed it, eyes boring into the man whose struggle intensified.

"What... what the hell are you?"

"I'm the guy who is going to make you watch me eat you unless you tell me where she is."

His throat bobbed as he swallowed hard and Dex willed himself not to watch. Not to imagine his Adam's apple slicing through the flesh and releasing the tantalizing scent of his blood into the air.

Dex tossed the dead man's arm aside and lifted the arm of the man trapped beneath him.

"Wait, wait, wait! Just wait!" he screamed. "Okay. Okay! She's inside. The basement. Kate's got her down there."

Kate. He committed the name to memory, knowing he would make her pay for whatever they were doing to Poe.

"So just... leave me be, you sick..." The words fell away and his eyes widened in regret. "I mean, just go on."

Shots rang out, and Dex's body jerked.

The front door to the mansion opened and men piled out. They were likely drawn out by the sound of shots.

Dex grinned.

Wonderful.

He started to get up, but paused long enough to rip the throat out of the man whose wrist was still in his grasp. Letting him live hadn't been one of the options.

He took his time standing and put the flesh in his hand in his mouth. Blood slid down his throat like a fine wine. "I believe you have something of mine," Dex purred.

"Do you have any idea whose house this is?" one of the men barked.

The thought he had earlier came to the forefront of his mind. "So long as she's under that roof, it's mine."

"The fuck it is!" Someone stepped forth and fired a shot.

Dex's shoulder flew back as the force of the bullet tore through him.

Darkness spread through his chest like the blood should have soaked through his shirt. His blood didn't do that, not anymore.

"Well." Dex dragged the pad of his thumb along his bottom lip, smearing it with blood. "I suppose when I'm standing over a pile of bodies, there will be no one left to argue that fact."

He lunged.

The stories were wrong. There was a speed behind his movements. A quickness linked to his immortality they often never mentioned. Mortals would fear those cursed to live the undead life of a zombie if they truly knew just how lifelike they were. How easily he blended with the hoard of mortal flesh bags who moved through this city. How strong he was. Fast. Hungry.

Rigor mortis was something that set into the limbs of the undead, and the curse carved on his bones was very much alive, so in turn, was he. It was the fuel that promised to never gift him the respite of death.

His hand ripped out the throat of the man to his right, while he collided with the one in the centre. His teeth sunk into his throat. He felt the stiffness of his larynx as he squeezed it between his teeth. Felt the heat cascade down his chin as he ripped it free. This was not a time to feed, it was a time to destroy. To lay his frigid hands on them and show them how easily he could deliver them to Death. How simple it was to steal something as frivolous as a mortal life away. Unnoticed in the dark of night. It was to awaken their fears and remind them that guns and knives were nothing when they stood face to face with a true monster.

His chest sheened as the moon reflected off the blood that dripped there. Coated his flesh. Seeped through the thin fabric of his shirt and made it cling to him.

A growl left him as he threw his head up and inhaled the night air. Let it blend with the blood in his mouth, flavour it.

A whimper stole his attention as the last man on the ground scurried back, fear in his eyes as they locked onto the arm Dex held in his hand. He didn't even remember tearing it off.

Thick tears rimmed the man's eyes, the gun in his hand forgotten as he huddled back against the door. He wore a satisfying look of terror as his lips quivered and his chin wrinkled. "What are you?" his voice cracked under the weight of his dread.

"Can't you recognize a monster when you see one?" Dex pulled the severed arm back, and brought it down again and again, until the sound of flesh against flesh grew moist and the man's whimpering ceased.

With the broken and bloodied arm in his hand, Dex pulled open the front door and walked in.

17
POE

HER PAIN MADE TIME feel pointless. There was no tick of seconds, no stretch of minutes, no way to tell the hour. Everything happened all at once just as it stretched on for an eternity. She could live in her pain. Exist there without the promise of an end and with no way of telling where it all began. So different from her need and hunger that kept time. Knew when night fell and she needed to feed.

It gave her far too much time to think.

To remember back to the first moment she ever set eyes on the zombie who infected her without biting her. Who captivated her and made her this obsessive thing that existed to dream up a life for him. To capture photos of him. To forever follow behind him.

It was winter.

Poe didn't understand people's dislike of the winter. In Toronto, the winters had a bite that spread misery. Heavy foot traffic that mushed unshovelled snow into a slush that immediately soaked into boots. That damp chill bit into toes. The high towers created wind tunnels that carried snowflakes like daggers in the wind. They sliced at frigid cheeks, bit at noses.

She loved the winter. Love the misery it brought with it.

Dex seemed like he liked it too. She remembered thinking that as she watched him walk in cool air with his feet sunk in the heavy snow and his winter coat open. His hands were in his pockets, but he hadn't bothered with a hat or scarf. Like he invited the winter in along with its misery.

It charmed her as she wandered through the busy city in nothing but a thick sweater, toque and boots better suited for the rain than the harsh winters. She began following him that day and never stopped. She followed him right up to tonight in the garage, where she followed him straight into her heartbreak.

Drip, drip, drip.

Her blood was the only thing that kept her from being completely lost in her memories. From feeling the blow of wind against her cheeks, the kind that numbed the tips of her fingers. From hearing the crunch of snow beneath her boots.

Being immortal was a curious thing.

With all the blood that slicked the tarp under the chair she still allowed herself to be bound to, she should have none left. She should be nothing but a hollowed husk, with no life left to keep her heart's beating. Yet... the smallest drop of magic would always be enough to sustain her.

Her fangs vibrated in her jaw with yearning. They wanted to bite, wanted to suck a soul from its casing and rejuvenate the flesh that felt so very mortal tonight. Not because of the onslaught of torment that had her captors wiping at their brow, but because she wasn't sure Dex would come.

She'd laughed at them. Told them how easily he could kill them all, but as she sat there, she wasn't sure if he would kill for her.

It made her ache.

Her arm hung like dead weight from her shoulder. Dislocated. She barely noticed the pain as she lightly giggled to herself, wondering just what her father would do if he could see her here, like this at the hands of mortals. He had no repugnance directed at the humans. As a reaper, he was a neutral being. He neither loved nor despised them. They merely were, and he chaperoned their souls to Death when their lives were done, just as he did all other beings in existence. Still, he would summon a passion they were unknown for as he laid his hands on them. Show them the force of his ire as he shook his head at the way she sat there, accepting the affliction they offered.

Her mother would have already clouded their minds with lust. Climbed out of the chair before they landed a single blow and created an orgy on the tarp that should have been covered with her blood.

The knowledge that her parents would have reacted to this situation so differently from her just drove the lonely point that she was both of them as much as she was neither.

The taste of her blood was suddenly bitter on her tongue. The dried blood that caked her skin in certain places made it feel too tight.

"We've played with her enough." Brick wiped her blood from his hands as he spoke. "If Fiona really is dead, we have shit to do."

The malice on Kate's face was delicious. It made Poe wish she'd gotten the chance to throw her in her bed. To see if that passion was as raw and unforgiving as her bloodthirst. "Her father will want her head."

Jake rubbed his bloodied hands together. "Let's give it to him then."

Tate ran a hand across his brow. Her blood on his pale skin looked sinister and made him all the more attractive. Death had a way of painting someone in a beauty very few would ever get to see, too blinded by their fear. Death was a beautiful thing. More breathtaking than any piece of art. Rife with emotions so raw, it tore most open. Bared their insides to the world.

He disappeared from sight for a moment before he returned with a machete. "I'm getting tired of this, anyway. Let's finish this up. I have shit to do."

"*We* have shit to do," Jake agreed.

"Are you about to keep your promise," Poe taunted. She wondered just what would happen if they decapitated her. She'd been shot, stabbed, even burned. Beheading would be new. She wasn't entirely sure how she'd survive it, she only knew she would.

It was due time for a new adventure, she supposed.

A part of her wished it took a while. If she didn't instantly recover from losing her head — physically, mentally it was already gone — she could busy herself trying to figure it out. Forget the pain in her chest that still made everything else they'd done to her feel numb in comparison.

Tate pulled the blade back, and Poe readied herself. "Yes. We told you we'd kill you."

"I give you an A for your effort."

"Fucking cheeky thing. I would have loved to get my hands on her if she hadn't been Fiona's killer. There's something special about the ones that are slightly unhinged. A hunger that takes forever to sate." Tate sighed. "What a fucking waste."

"Oh, I don't know. I would never call a learning experience a waste. You've all done great work here. The whole electrocution thing was a fun change. I was bored of being shot. It's all kind of the same. Hot, tearing pain. Blah, blah, blah." Poe rolled her eyes as she spoke. "The fingernails was kind of fun too. I never thought they'd come off so easily."

He swung the blade.

Most would have clenched their eyes closed. As though closed eyes would somehow shut out the pain that followed. They would throw themself in the nothingness behind their lids hoping the nothingness death brought would be just as swift. Just as painless as a shut of their eyes. Poe kept her eyes open. She wanted to see it. Wanted to watch and accept the misery that would be delivered to her. Afraid she might miss it.

Poe wanted to bear witness.

The smirk on her face was a taunt. She knew it only intensified Tate's want to remove her head. Good. She was suddenly curious about what she would look like without her head. The image of the Headless Horseman came to mind, and she smiled at the possibility of haunting a neighbourhood in the city. Likely this gated one with the Toronto Elites thinking they were safe behind their gates and walls.

But where would she get a ghost horse?

Did the headless horseman's horse die too? Or... what was the story there?

She honestly didn't remember.

It couldn't be that hard to figure out. In a world of immortal beings, one of them had to have an undead horse. She had a zombie lover — for however brief a time — clearly nothing was impossible.

She'd name him Figaro. Or Biscuits... she liked biscuits.

Hmm, but that wasn't very scary.

Grimm, she decided. After her father.

Surprise transformed Tate's face. His head whipped to the side, and he was face to face with the very zombie that drove her here.

Dex.

His hand wrapped around the back of Tate's neck, grip unforgiving. Dex wrapped his other hand around Tate's wrist, the force kept Tate from bringing the machete down on her neck. Dex tore the blade from his grasp and whipped it behind him. The blade impaled Brick's shoulder and pinned him to the wall behind him.

The stoic look on Brick's face was gone as he reached out and tried to pry the blade free. His jaw clenched in obvious pain.

The doubtful place in the centre of her chest that leaked sadness and regret was appeased by the sight of him. The cracks in her mind slightly soothed at knowing he came. For her. Just like she hoped he would. "How wonderful," Poe sighed.

Jake held his hand out and kept Kate behind him as he raised his gun.

A shot rang through the air, but she ignored it as Dex lowered Tate toward her.

"A bite, Poe," he offered.

Time slowed.

It felt silly to say. To admit everything else in the room blurred away to nothing, her vision dark at the edges as she met the tortured face of her zombie. His skin slightly paled with those black veins darkening his face at the edges. His lips were so red, the scent of death so heady on him it made her mouth water.

Another shot rang out, but it was muffled. It could have been a kilometre away for all she knew.

Tate squirmed in his grasp, but Dex held her gaze with his. The morbid look in his eyes was enticing with their milky hue. "Eat. Heal. Then create havoc with me, beautiful monster."

Her mouth opened. Tate's eyes widened, but she ignored him as Dex pulled his head to the side and she sunk her teeth into Tate's throat.

The bite of death was a sweet one. It filled her senses so completely, she hummed as the elixir of life moved through her. Set her veins alight. Stitched the skin they'd worked so hard to split and break. Realigned the bones.

Tate's struggling ceased, and Dex dropped his body to the floor.

"What the fuck?" Murmured panic sounded so far away.

Poe pulled against the cuffs, felt the way they broke from the legs of the chair, and lifted her hands to cup Dex's face. He leaned in, as desperate to feel her touch as she was to give it.

Her fingers brushed through the blood on his cheeks, thumbs slowly traced his bottom lip as her eyes moved back and forth between his. "You came."

"For you. Always."

Her heart fluttered in her chest.

This was romance. As dark as it seemed, covered in blood and stinking of death, this was the story of romance she would have written for herself, staring at his photo in one of her countless frames.

Another shot.

Poe chuckled and rolled her eyes. "Mortals are silly things," she whispered. No bigger truth had been told. He hadn't reacted to the first few shots, and still they tried again and again. Sought out no new solutions.

"Tasty, silly things," he agreed. His hand reached around her neck, his thumb lightly traced the bite mark that hadn't quite healed. "Have you fed enough?"

She couldn't say. Everything melted away, and all that existed was Dex.

"Poe."

His voice was beautiful. She wanted him to whisper sweet nothings in her ear. Tangle his fingers in her hair, his nails against her scalp as he spoke of all the things they'd do together. It was the sweetest melody. A serenade that would always bring her to her knees.

"Poe."

"Hmm?"

Dex's hands ran over her newly freed arms. His touch was painfully soft as it ran over her bruised flesh. It made behind her eyes burn and confusion flip her stomach. "Have you fed enough?"

The room came back into view and she looked at Jake over Dex's shoulder. Hate was heavy in his eyes as he lifted a knife over Dex's head.

The cuffs around her ankles and wrists crumbled like wet paper as she pulled against them. Her hands wrapped around the spikes in her legs and effortlessly pulled them free. On her feet, she slammed a spike through his raised wrist. A howl left him as he dropped the knife. Her smirk spread wide as she watched his fear take hold. "Is this where you kill me?"

The promises they made her were ones she knew wouldn't be kept, but she wanted to see the realization hit him. Wanted him to acknowledge she was right.

Jake jerked his hand, but it went nowhere. Poe was too strong. She yanked him toward her, mouth open and at the ready. Her teeth sunk into him before he could do anything about it.

Satisfaction filled her, and her eyes rolled back in her head. As haunted as she was by the affliction of her unpredictable magic, there was nothing that filled her so completely as souls. At least there wasn't — until Dex.

A whimper left Kate. Her hand shook as she held her gun raised. Wide eyes looked down at the husk of Tate before they flew up to Jake, still held up by Poe. "What — what the fuck are you people?"

Poe dropped Jake and stepped over his body. They looked beautiful in the backdrop of all the blood they'd stolen from her. Pale bodies in a sea of red.

Her movements toward Kate were slow, but her shaky hand never pulled the trigger. Her fear wouldn't let her. Not without an explanation. She needed to know. Needed something to explain the fear away.

"Us?" Teeth bared, she hissed at Kate. "We're monsters."

Poe lunged at her.

The taste of Kate's soul wasn't as sweet as it would have been if it had followed the appetizer of lust. If she had a taste of the twisted desires Kate hid inside. It would do though. It always did.

Kate's hands clutched around Poe's arms. So close to an embrace, she could fool herself and pretend it was, until the life left her grip and her hands sagged at her sides. Her head lobbed lightly as her weight fell into Poe's firm hold.

Dead.

No reaper to collect her. There was no soul left to take.

Poe ran her tongue along her lips, tasting the blood she left behind as the warmth of Dex's arms wrapped around her middle and pulled her back against his chest. Her head fell back. "You're lucky you came. I wouldn't have forgiven your foolishness otherwise."

"Aren't all men fools?" He dropped his head and ran the roughness of his cheek against her own as he inhaled her.

"Until the day they die... so you have no excuse." He really didn't. An immortal life that ran parallel to eternity should have given him knowledge enough not to so thoroughly piss her off.

His chuckle was a sound she sorely missed in the short time they'd been parted. "Fair enough. But you *have* forgiven me?"

Poe thought about it. She wasn't some thoughtless damsel. She could have escaped at any time. Snapped those cuffs and took the souls from them just as easily as she just had without Dex's assistance. She'd waited for him, longed for someone to care enough to rescue her.

And he had.

That only kept the door open.

"No." She wouldn't forgive him, not yet. He hadn't earned it.

His hold tightened, and she revelled in the feel of his arms. "No?"

"No. That's too easy."

"What then? What do I have to do to prove to you I would apologize until my voice was hoarse and the last breath left me?"

Poe considered. That would take far too long, and she had no use for words. "I'm part succubus, and all this death without the lust to chase it makes my skin feel like it's on fire."

His bloodied hand slid down, lifted the hem of her short dress, and ran his fingers slowly up the inside of her thigh. "Is heat not something a succubus enjoys unless it's heat she creates?"

A low moan came from her throat as his fingers brushed against the lips of her pussy. He painted them with the havoc they created here before he dipped them inside her. She moaned again, her back arched as she pressed more of herself into him.

As with everything where Dex was concerned, he kept a brutal pace. Two of his thick fingers moved while his thumb pressed against her clit, a button that made her insides coil and her thighs shake.

"Tell me, my beautiful monster, will you come for me? Soak my fingers? Wash away the blood with a wave of your pleasure." His hand moved quickly as he asked his questions. His face dropped, his teeth nipping at her ear.

The sharp slice of pain was all it took. The scent of death around them was exhilarating, like smoke in the air that clouded her mind and muffled her senses. Her eyes rolled back as she tightened, a fragile cord pulled between his capable fingers, and then snapped.

He lifted her face, sealing their lips together. Bitter bliss coated her tongue, entrancing in its intensity. Blood and pleasure.

Her orgasm was more intense that her torture. It ripped out of her, made her flesh buzz. No bite was needed. Dex was the taste of death and he was heavy on her tongue.

Dex's grip tightened around her as he breathed into her ear. Each breath a ragged thing he had to force himself to keep under control. "Again," he growled.

"You're in no place to demand anything from me," she mumbled, voice heavy with lust.

"I will demand your pleasure until the day you die."

"Mmm." That thought made her grin, knowing just how long he would have to demand it. "I crave more."

"More?"

Her hand reached between them, tightened over the crotch of his slacks. "More."

Dex released her, but only long enough to turn her to face him. He lifted her, dropped to his knees to lay her on the bloodied tarp at their feet. His hand fisted in her panties as her legs parted and he tore them between her legs.

Poe reached out, fumbling with his belt. She never really liked belts. She enjoyed removing them. Liked the sound the buckle made as it tried to do its job, but her fingers refused to let it, but hated the task. She wanted to get to her prize quickly. Wanted to see what she would get to devour. To ride.

She freed him and licked her lips. The thought of the thick length of him inside her made her stomach flutter and her heart quicken.

Lined up, Dex dragged a hand over the side of her face. "All the things I've wanted to do to you, keeping you is the one that I know I can't deny."

A grunt stole their attention.

They both gazed up at Brick, still pinned to the wall. He fought against the blade that was sunk too deep to escape it, whipped with a strength well beyond what he would ever be capable of.

The detached look of him was rattled. She'd pulled the thread when she took Tate's soul and hadn't let it go, causing him to unravel as she did it to Jake and then to Kate. As he watched just how close he'd stood to a monster, how he gifted her his blows, unknowing of just what she could take from him. With very little effort.

"Oh, I almost forgot about Brick."

"Let him watch." Dex dropped his face and inhaled her before he pressed the heat of his lips to her throat and thrust forward.

She was filled to bursting. He paused, letting her adjust to the stretch he caused, the blissful ache that made her pulse and whine for more. Her head rolled back, eyes on the man pinned to the wall forced to watch them fuck surrounded by the bodies of his friends.

Her heart quickened.

"Do you forgive me now?" Dex asked.

"Fuck me right, and we'll talk about it." Poe grinned.

Dex moved.

This was not the slow tempo of love making. It was not a choreographed, beautiful thing that captivated and drew tears. It was quick and forceful. It was thrusts that made her slide against the tarp with their strength. Violence surrounded by violence. Brutal and magnificent. Her hands slid against the heated moisture pooled around her, collected it, before she smeared them over his back.

Her slick hands clung to him, her heels wrapped under his ass.

"Harder," she begged.

If he fucked her any harder, he'd fuck her through the floor. She felt the slam of cement against her back and the shot of pain it created. It made her giggle, a sound that turned into a moan as he rolled his hip and he rubbed against her clit with each thrust. The sound of the tarp rustling under them and the slap of skin was like a shot of luxuria straight to her veins. It built up her need, her succubus wild inside her as it begged for more.

"Dex," she groaned.

"Come for me, beautiful monster. Scream for me."

He rose on his knees, hands wrapped around her upper thighs as he lifted her so her shoulders were the only thing pressed against the ground. The change of angle made her head spin. Each vicious slam of his hips hit off something inside her that made her see stars.

"Fuck," she hissed through her teeth.

"Come for me," he demanded. One hand slipped behind her back to lift her into his chest.

Poe clung to him, her arms wrapped around his neck as she lifted herself, only to slam down again and again onto him. "I—" A sharp breath stole her words, not that she had any to give him. She couldn't think beyond her pleasure, beyond the wave of lust that seeped into her every pore like chocolate, decadent and sweet.

"Bite me, Poe. Mark me as yours."

Her mouth was open as soon as he asked, her teeth pressed into the side of his neck. She ran her tongue over him, the taste of his flesh sticky and metallic.

Dex groaned, his grip on her so tight she could feel the imprint of his nails on her hips. "Bite me, please. Make me yours. Make me yours this time and every time after. Please."

Her heart clenched in the tight grip of his words. It felt like an admission of love, only no one loved her. Not really.

Right?

Her teeth sank into his skin and his thrust became erratic. Poe held on. The taste of him — of death — and the feel of him buried so deep inside her more than she could bear.

She wanted to tell him she was going to come, but couldn't bring herself to pull her teeth from his flesh. She didn't want to let him go. Not now. Not ever.

She felt herself tighten. Her inner walls held onto him, made him work to leave her only to enter her again.

He was hers, and she wouldn't allow any take backs.

A growl left him just as she jumped over the edge, and her orgasm took hold. Her legs quaked, everything in her tightened as her clit tingled and she soaked him. Felt the moisture, hot and steady, as it poured out of her to drip on the tarp below.

Dex's head dropped to her shoulder, his own teeth edged against her skin before he pressed a kiss there. Wet heat filled her, the gentle throb of his cock hinting his release. She tightened the grip of her jaw and let the euphoric swell of her magic flood through him. A groan left him. Her magic made more cum surge into her. It filled her until it dripped out, his lethargic thrusts forcing it from her. It sent her own orgasm into overdrive. Curled her toes and made thick tears roll down the side of her face.

"There is no heart in my chest without you. Do you understand that, Poe? Do you understand that before you, I was cursed bones covered in flesh. No purpose. No respite to my torment."

A tired chuckle left her as she clung to him. "I'll offer you no respite to your torment, Dex. I imagine I'll do just the opposite."

"Hmm." The hum was a lazy agreement. "But how wonderful a torment you'll be, beautiful monster."

"The wicked kind that bites."

"Your bite brings the most euphoric kind of pain."

"You sick fucks!" Brick spat. "Fucking messed in the head, both of you."

Dex's hand left her long enough to scoop the knife off the floor.

"We'll kill you, you know that, don't you? They'll never stop. Not until the two of you are dead. You think they don't see you? That we don't have cameras all over this place? They know your faces now. Know who you are." Brick's angry words meant nothing.

A flick of Dex's wrist, and the blade sunk between Brick's eyes.

His head slumped forward and Poe's inner walls tightened. They squeezed the cock still inside her, not yet soft.

Dex groaned. "Fuck, Poe. You're going to be the death of me, aren't you?"

Lifting herself slowly, her breath hitched and her eyes rolled back. "I guess it's a good thing you're already dead."

18

A S MACABRE AS HE was, he could only lay with Poe surrounded by death for so long before he scooped her up and went in search of a bathroom.

He held her in his arms as he walked through the house, leaving a trail of bloodied footprints behind him. She threw her head back, ever dramatic as she ran her hands along the walls, touched every banister, painting or bust they passed. She hummed to herself as they made their way through, a content smile on her face and her eyes wild.

"So much space. How ever will we find our way?" she sang.

"I'll just keep opening doors until we find the one with a shower behind it." He tightened his grip on her, lifting her slightly to press a gentle kiss to her temple.

His heart thrummed so hard in his chest it made his ribs hurt.

"Good call." Poe clicked her tongue. Her eyes looked down over the bloodied mess that was her skin. Her mouth pursed before she let out a long sigh. "I could really use a playlist for this cleanup."

Dex's brow quirked. "A playlist? You have a playlist for this?"

"I have a playlist for everything. Body clean up. Digging. Fucking. Seduction. Anger. Sadness. You know... normal stuff."

There was nothing even remotely normal about Poe. That was what he loved about her.

It took three doors before he found a bathroom. Massive and luxurious. He stepped onto the marble floors and looked at the framed walls and claw-foot tub. He carried her in, looking over everything in shades of whites. Dex didn't release her as he turned on the tub and sat her on its edge.

On his knees, he pressed a kiss to her lips. It was meant to be chaste. Quick. But her teeth captured his bottom lip and punctured his skin. His cock bobbed as her magic poured into him. A lust so intoxicating it made his head spin.

"It feels weird... to feel so alive." Since the first time he laid his hands on her, he felt *mortal*. His heart raced, butterflies flit through his stomach, his throat tightened and his mouth went dry. He was a teen again, caught in a whirlwind of emotions he hadn't the faculties to control.

Like his emotions were bigger than him, and he couldn't contain them. Couldn't keep them from bursting out of him.

Dex reached up to tear her dress. When she was bare, he stood, quickly stripping out of his own clothes. He lifted her again, stepping into the tub. He watched the water turn pink around their legs before he lowered himself to sit.

Poe settled in front of him, her chest to his and her legs over his hips.

They sat there and just stared at one another.

He turned off the tap and let the silence envelop them. Caught in the sight of her, wanting nothing more than to stare at the amazing woman he'd somehow managed to catch and hold on to. A woman who seemed as obsessed with him as he was with her.

As impossible as it seemed, there she was. Sullying the water right alongside him.

Her hands reached up and traced the line of his brow. "I don't belong," she whispered.

"You belong to me," he said easily.

"No." She smiled lightly but shook her head. "That's not what I mean. I mean, I don't belong in any realm. I've no wings. No dreamscape. So I can't exist in my mother's realm where succubi find home in the shadows. I can't reap souls. Can't deliver them to Death. I can't even find my way to him or move through existence to the souls that sometime whisper to me. I don't belong. Which means, often, my voice is stifled. What can I know about being a succubus? What can I know about being a reaper?"

It pained him to know she felt this way. A puzzle piece with smooth edges that didn't fit in worlds she clearly wished she did.

"You stifled my voice, Dex."

Those words were like she reached through his flesh and tore out the very heart she brought back to life.

"Back in my garage. I told you I was fine, and you just ignored me. You just looked through me and ran out. Like what I had to say didn't matter. Like *I* didn't matter." Her bottom lip poked out. He wanted to capture it, but didn't want to distract from the solemnity of their conversation.

He brought his finger up under her chin and pulled her face gently up to meet his. He saw the way her eyes glistened with tears she wouldn't shed. "Poe," he said, his voice heavy with remorse.

"Don't do that to me. Not you."

He'd been irrational in the garage. He knew that. Their relationship up to that point had been an obsession neither of them surrendered to — and passion. Poe hadn't had the chance to see him as he was. As the curse made him. When he'd bit her, he'd been afraid of what that would cost her, what it would cost *them*. Afraid what the true sight of him as a zombie would mean.

Ignoring what she'd had to say about it hurt her, and that made him irritated with himself.

"I'm so sorry, Poe. That wasn't my intention. I just..." He sighed. "I was too caught up in my own thoughts, I didn't pause long enough to think about yours."

Her nod was slow, but her eyes were fierce. "Don't do that to me again, do you understand?"

"I won't." And he wouldn't. He would do whatever it took to make sure she never wore the look she did now, directing it at him in a way that sliced open his chest and made his heart bleed.

She pointed an accusing finger at him, that adorable knot between her eyes creased as she lifted the corner of her upper lip and made one of her fangs visible. "If you do it again, I will be forced to punish you."

"Oh?" A smile touched his lips at all the sinful possibilities.

"Don't get excited. It won't be a punishment you'll enjoy, you pervert."

"I find that hard to believe." He doubted there was something she could do to him he couldn't find a way to enjoy.

Poe shimmied closer. Dex bit down on her lower lip as he felt her rub against his length. Tease him in a way only she could. Her grip shifted, her hand wrapped around his jaw as she jerked his face toward hers. "My handsome, undead obsession. As much as I love you, I don't like being hurt by people I care about. It makes me a villainous thing. I welcome the agony those who don't matter to me can bring, use it to spice up an endless life with no finish line in sight, but when I care about someone and they hurt me... I can't control the way my wicked mind reacts." Her grip tightened, the pointed ends of her nails pierced his skin. "I will be forced to hurt you back to appease the parts of my heart that don't know any better. No. Actually, they do. They know better, but long for the wretched way it soothes the aches you caused."

"I'd gladly accept any punishment you offered. I'd take what I deserve and love you still." The word slipped out so freely, he hadn't known it was coming. Like it belonged to her, just as he did. Something she took so long ago, carved her name into, that he hadn't considered the implications of it before he set it loose from his tongue.

That unhinged smile, a tad too wide, that set all her teeth on display stretched across her face. "You love me, ghoulie?"

He rolled his eyes at the nickname. "Yes."

"Like..." She rolled her hips again. "A lot?"

"Mark my days and my nights as yours, beautiful monster, they'll never belong to another."

"Because you love me?"

He wished there was a word that meant more to give her, if only to see if he could make her smile all the more vibrant. All the more twisted and sinister and his. "More than I've ever loved anything else. We're both cursed, you and I. How something that plagued us could be such a gift now, realizing it makes us perfect for each other."

Poe looked up at the ceiling in thought. "Huh. I never really thought about it like that."

"And now that you have?"

"Now that I have, I'm debating whether I should stop calling my mother a whore whenever I'm slightly inconvenienced." Poe let out a dramatic huff and shook her head. "No, it's too fun and I like to think she can hear me."

Dex chuckled. "I'm sure she enjoys the endless barbs you stick her with."

Poe nodded, face suddenly serious. "She does. I'm sure of it. If there is one thing my mother wears proudly, it's her body count... and not in the same way I do. With the whole *devouring souls* thing."

"Would you say you take after your mother?" he asked, suddenly curious about her roots. He wondered if her mother was as untamed and slightly delirious as Poe was. He had a feeling she didn't get any of her personality from her father. Reapers were usually apathetic and a tad dull.

"She wishes," Poe scoffed before she let her hands drop to trail down Dex's chest.

"Do you forgive me yet?" he asked. It was meant to be something asked in jest, but the tightness in his throat as he waited for the answer told him it mattered. That despite their banter, he needed her to say the words. To forgive him.

"Almost. I'm not so easy, Dex. You'll have to work for it."

"Is that right?"

"Yes," she affirmed. "That's right. Count yourself lucky. My first thought was to bury you and make you beg for days and days. Only digging you up when you were in a state to completely ravish me."

Dex's brows dropped. "I can ravish you without you keeping me in a box."

"I'm sure you could, but then it wouldn't be a punishment. I'd sit on your grave and force you to listen to me come over and over and over and make you wonder if I'm by myself up there or—"

Nostrils flared, he jerked Poe closer to him and lined himself up with her entrance. "You're a mischievous thing, aren't you, beautiful monster?"

"In a morbid way I'm sure will suit you perfectly." Poe grinned at him before she took his lips with her own and sunk down on him.

"Perfectly," he agreed.

19

POE

LIFE SUDDENLY BECAME FILLED with colour. She'd heard people talk about the *Honeymoon Phase* before, but never knew what it could mean. With Dex's hand in hers and that twisted smile on his face, the one that lit his dark eyes and tightened her stomach and the space between her thighs, she felt a bliss she wasn't entirely sure couldn't be caused by magic. Weeks were spent sharing cups of coffee in her kitchen, dancing to music through her house, tangled in her sheets, cuddled together, watching movies they never made it through — their clothes on the floor and their hands all over one another — and hunting the people who hunted her.

Her life was more than she dared hoped it ever could be. She had the man she lusted after in her bed. The very one that cooled her succubus blood, wracked her body with orgasms unassisted by blood and soul. A man she could bite without the risk of devouring his soul. Dex's soul wasn't a reaper's to deliver — or devour.

He was as safe from her as she was from him. His bites ones that would always heal. The taste of her blood enough to sate him.

They walked through the cemetery, muffled cursing coming from the abandoned mausoleum ahead. Every now and again, the twisted parts of them longed for flesh in their teeth, for souls slipped down her throat. Not for the relief it used to bring, but for the satisfaction. In knowing the person under their hands deserved all they brought.

When she brought that quick lay, Adam, back to her place, she never imagined he would be tied to so many ruthless people with blackened souls. A hum sounded as she danced around the graves, her hands above her head as she twirled in the moonlight. Dex captured her hand, spinning her before he dropped her into a dip. Poe giggled. Her hand reached up to brush the flat of her palm against the rough stubble against his jaw.

"How many times do I have to tell you, you don't have to dance alone anymore?" Dex pressed his lips against hers, stealing a kiss.

He always tasted so good. Like freedom. Dreams she'd finally captured. Beautiful nightmares that tortured her but felt so damned good while they did.

He lifted her, his hands tightly cupped her sides as he did. "Ready?"

"Almost." Poe leapt into his arms, wrapping her legs around his waist. "Now I am."

"I'm meant to carry you then?" Dex chuckled low, his face immediately finding that space between her neck and shoulder that plummeted her that much deeper into her madness.

Thighs tensed around his hips, she stretched out her leg and wiggled her bare toes. "I'm not wearing any shoes."

He huffed a breath, and another laugh left him. "Where are your shoes, beautiful monster?"

Poe thought about it. She really wasn't sure. She'd had them once, but she couldn't really remember when that was. Her thoughts were too preoccupied with visions of Dex between her legs, coaxing orgasms out of her like it was his job, biting into her flesh and running the chill of his tongue against the sensitive flesh of her thighs.

"Poe?"

"Hmm." She snapped her attention back to him.

"Where are your shoes?" he asked again.

"What are shoes when you're in the arms of a zombie that is going to devour your pussy as thoroughly as he's going to devour the asshole we left tied up in the mausoleum? Hmm?" she challenged. How the hell did he expect her to stay on task when the stakes were so high? When she knew just how thick and heavy his cock was, how well it hit that spot inside her that made her see stars and surrender all she was to him. All she would ever be.

Dex pressed a kiss to her temple as he carried her toward the mausoleum. "True enough. Though, as tempting as you are and always will be to me, I'm wearing shoes."

Her eyes dropped down to his feet, clad in comfortable trainers. "And that's why you're the one doing the carrying."

"You'd carry me if I misplaced my shoes?" She loved when his voice sounded humourous as it did now. Loved knowing she brought so much joy into his life, he could barely contain it.

She nuzzled her face into his neck. "Yup. I would carry you off into the sunset."

Dex tightened his hold on her as he opened the door to the mausoleum and stepped into the damp, dimly lit tomb. It was lit by dozens of candles, the plaques on the little drawers, worn away, reflected the light. He carried her in, walking toward the man gagged and bound by the small cross set in stained glass windows. It had been a long time since anyone used this place. The stone vases set in the floor around the cross were homes to critters, likely with no memory of what it felt like to be filled with flowers.

He didn't urge her to get down as they reached the man at their — his — feet. He adjusted his stance, but Poe wiggled down him and set her feet on the floor. Dex's hand rested possessively on her hip as he glared down at the man. "Just how many people are looking for Fiona?"

They'd left the other bodies behind to be found. Well, most of them.

The man mumbled under his gag, and Poe sighed. "Speak up, will ya?" She squatted and pulled the gag from his mouth. He snarled at her, lunging to nip at her hand. "Such a grumpy guy," she sassed.

Dex kicked him. "You take a bite out of her, I take a bite out of you? And you won't like my bite." He snapped his teeth at him.

"Fuck you," the man spat.

Poe giggled. "Oh, I'll get to that later." She winked at Dex over her shoulder. "Right now, all we need to know is just how many people are planning to hunt me down for killing Adam and Fiona and..." She snapped her fingers, trying to think of the third person's name. "Trevor."

"Trent! His name was Trent, you fucking monster."

"Oh, right." Poe snapped her fingers again. "Trent. Such a forgettable name. He should change it." Trent, Tate, Kate... holy hell, it was hard to keep them all straight.

The man's eyes widened before they narrowed in anger. "He's dead."

"Semantics."

"Semantics," he repeated in disbelief. "*Semantics?*" His voice was shrill.

Poe covered her ears with her hands. "Yes. Christ, no need to shout."

"What the fuck is wrong with you? Are you out of your fucking mind? You killed over ten people. Now you want me to tell you how many are out for your head because of it. No way. I hope they come for you. I hope they rip your fingernails out one by one and make you eat them, you psychotic bitch!"

Lips pursed, Poe pouted. "Well, that's not very nice. Plus, they already did that." Aside from the eating them part.

Dex squat beside her. He pressed a kiss to her head before he untied the man's hands. Dex caught his wrist when he swung at Dex as soon as he was free, his other hand wrapped around its opposite as he looked it over with a hunger that ignited her own.

Poe sat back on her heels, her thighs clenched together. This was about to get *so* good.

The man yanked against Dex's hold but it was no use.

Dex bit into him.

The screams were so loud.

Poe stood, her hands waved in front of her like she was a conductor and this was her orchestra. The stone floors were cool on the soles of her feet. Dead leaves littered the area. They crunched under her feet, adding to the macabre sound. She swayed her hips, eyes closed as she danced to the sound of his screams and the gnash of Dex's teeth.

"Stop!" the man begged.

She hoped he didn't as much as she knew he had to. They needed information. Needed to know just how many more would come. Or, at least that was what Dex told her they needed. She much preferred to be surprised. To spend each day unknowing if someone would come up behind her and slice her throat. Inject her with blissful pain. Set her zombie wild with possessive protectiveness.

Dex allowed her to be just who she was, but offered a voice of reason. Whether she took it was always up to her.

The anger that built in him knowing someone might be out there hunting her made her give in. Being bait had been fun. Catching the man whose screams sounded so sweet had been even funner.

His cries turned to whimpers and sobs. Snot filled things, moist and disgusting. "You... you just—" a sob choked him and stole his words. "What the fuck are you?"

It was a question they'd gotten often. Poe not as often as Dex. Her bite stole the opportunity to ask questions away from them. Their soul in her gluttonous belly and their questions dead alongside them. Dex though... he looked into the eyes of the people he devoured lately. When it became clear they were after Poe, he wanted to make them suffer. Make them bleed for her.

"What is so important about Fiona? Why are they still looking for Poe?" Dex asked.

With her song over and no use for her talents, she turned to watch Dex drag his thumb over his bloodied bottom lip. The man's wrist was still in his grasp, but a chunk of his forearm was missing. She could see right down to the bone. A sheen of sweat made the man's brow shine as his eyes rolled back, head too heavy for his shoulders. "Do you even know who she is?" His words slurred. He was going to pass out any minute.

Pity.

"Who?" Dex prompted. "Tell me."

"Fiona Rinaldi."

The name was supposed to mean something. Dex looked back at her, and she shrugged. She didn't really understand the meaning behind names. Why would she? She'd chosen her own. Needed one to exist in the mortal realm. Poe had been the name given to her by her father, but Wiley was the surname she chose to go with it. Somehow, Grimm felt overused.

Plus, she was really wily.

She rarely paid attention to people's surnames. Fiona could have been Fiona Grimm for all Poe was concerned.

"Of the Rinaldi crime family." He had to push each word past his lips.

"That means something?" Dex asked.

"They're very big on weapons and drugs. Not the most powerful family in Toronto by any means, but powerful enough to make your life..." He swallowed hard. "A living hell."

Her smile became downright giddy. "A living hell. That sounds like fun."

Dex smiled but shook his head at her. "Fun, so long as you don't get hurt."

A pout plumped her lips. "But the pain is half the fun."

A scowl darkened his face, and she grabbed at her chest, letting a dramatic sigh leave her. "Is that look for me?"

"I'm a tad frustrated, Poe." He quickly made a correction. "Not at you."

"They'll come for you." The fatigue in his voice made it sound so far away. "They won't stop until you're dead."

Poe threw her weight onto Dex's back. Her arms wrapped around his neck, palms rested against his chest as she grinned over his shoulder. "Well, then I guess it's a good thing Dex is already dead. And me..." She pressed a kiss to the side of Dex's throat, where the scar of her bite was welted and raised. "You could say I'm Death's estranged granddaughter he has no intention of meeting. The nerve of that guy, right?"

His weight fell to the floor, his breath angry pants that inflated his chest.

"They're such weak little things," Poe complained. "I rarely get anything good from them before they pass out or die."

"I'd say that information was good." Dex threw the man's hand aside. "It would seem, beautiful monster, you took a bite out of someone mighty important. Someone who has an arsenal at their back and is going to come at you with a vengeful fury."

"Alexa!" She stood and moved to straddle Dex's lap. "Play my party playlist!"

"You think this is going to be a party?" He shook his head before he pressed a light kiss to her lips. "Also, you do realize we're in a mausoleum with no '*Alexa*', right?"

The thought of tearing through the city with her zombie lover and doing away with a whole crime family made her giddy with anticipation. This was most definitely a party, one of the funnest ones she would ever attend.

"I'm going to need a new dress. And boots... all good ass kicking happens in boots."

"Poe," he groaned.

"Hmm?"

"This is serious. You realize that, don't you?" His eyes bore into hers with a deep longing that made her stomach clench. "I don't want anything to happen to you."

She pressed their brows together. "Well, then it's a good thing you'll be around to make sure nothing does."

20

POE

T HREE MONTHS, TWO WEEKS, and four days. That's how long it took them to work their way through Rinaldi's syndicate up to the top. It was havoc. Those in Toronto who lived a mundane life free from crime and immortals were none the wiser of the blood that ran down their streets in the dark of night. Of the monsters on the hunt.

Dex was amazing. His blood thirst awoke something in her she hadn't thought was there. A craving that went beyond her lust or the taste of death. He awoke a need for chaos.

With her back pinned outside the walls of his office in an upscale home in some silly neighbourhood much like the one she was tortured in, she grinned over at Dex, who stood at the ready. He held a severed arm in his grasp, as though it were the only weapon he needed. Poe had gone with an abandoned gun, though she regret it now. She'd love to see the surprise on his face as she beat him to death with the arm of someone he once knew.

Hindsight was twenty-twenty.

A pout touched her lips for a moment before she willed it away.

Mortals found guns good enough, and they sure did their best to riddle her full of bullets. A gun seemed right for this.

A sad huff left her as she looked over at the zombie who stole her heart and held it in his chest alongside his own, cold and barely beating. "To the death." Poe winked, that unhinged smile stretched over her face.

"There's no death for us, beautiful monster." His eyes held a depth to them she got lost in every time he looked at her. How she longed to live inside the chasm of despair that often lived there.

"Well." Poe pursed her lips, brow quirked. "This is going to be really fun then!"

Dex kicked open the door and strut in. One hand in his pocket and the other holding the severed arm by the flesh he'd ripped out of the man's shoulder, the knuckles dragged lightly across the floor. Poe strut in behind him, the gun lowered at her side.

Her eyes looked over the room in its creams and rich browns. Whiskey leathers and teak woods. The far wall was all windows in thick framing. A large desk set in front of it with a burly man behind it. He sat in his chair, cigar in his mouth, and a handgun, much like the one in her own, held out. Salt and pepper hair brushed back from his brow, his olive skin as weathered as the leather.

His eyes widened slightly, so quickly they might have missed it, as he looked at the arm Dex held in his hand. His fear was a mere flash, but she saw it and it made her smile.

A long sigh left her as her hands went behind her back, and she lazily paced the room. "What is with you guys and your big houses? How many of these rooms do you actually use?"

Rude as he was — with the whole hunting her down and trying to kill her thing — he didn't answer her.

Poe walked over to the wall with a fireplace set in the middle and picked up a photo on the mantle. It was of Fiona. She held a cat pressed up to her cheek and smiled at the camera. She looked like a completely different woman than the one Poe met. Her chestnut brown hair was pulled back from her face. Make-up was light. For the briefest moment, Poe wondered what happened to the woman in the photo to transform her to the dark woman she met. The one who had malice in her eyes and with the twisted smile that hinted danger instead of the light the girl in the photo wore.

The one whose soul tasted of sin and sinister intentions.

Perhaps it was the man behind the desk.

"Your numbers are dwindling." Dex pulled out the chair on the other side of the desk and sank into it like he belonged there. His leg folded, ankle on his thigh as he threw the arm over his lap and looked at the man like he would someone beneath him. "We were going to continue on just cutting your numbers, but then a thought came to me. If I just kill you, then all your little henchmen should go away. At least, those with any sense would."

"And you think you can just kill Marcus Rinaldi?"

Dex clicked his tongue. "I'm almost positive that's exactly what I'll do."

Rinaldi leaned back in his chair, hard steel eyes on Poe despite Dex's closer position.

"After all the lives we've taken already, what makes you think we can't?" Poe turned to look at him, her elbow on the mantle. She saw her reflection in the window behind him, sinister beauty with her kinky curls wild and her brown skin splattered with blood. "What made you think you could win here?"

"It's not about winning. You stole from me."

"I steal from a lot of people," Poe confessed. "Souls are easy things to steal."

He shot up to his feet. "You killed my daughter."

"Yes," she admitted.

He lifted his gun.

The arm held in Dex's hand came up. Its hand slapped across Rinaldi's face. Dex ignored Rinaldi's surprised look and smacked him again, this time with enough force to send him back in his chair.

"I would warn you not to point that at her. I've killed people for a lot less."

Rinaldi's chuckle was sad. "Then you know why I do this. Why I will sacrifice whatever I have to in order to bring my daughter's murderer to their knees before me."

It was a sad thing to admit she understood. If anyone dared do anything to Dex, she would burn the world to the ground to make them pay. Damn everyone who got in her way. She would darken the world just as his loss would darken hers.

In this room stood three dark souls. One who lived a life of crime. Peddled drugs and weapons into their city. Broke fingers and fired shots at those who defied him. One who ate flesh to appease a curse that stole all the feelings from his limbs. And her, maybe the worst villain of them all. Someone who devoured the souls of those she infused with a lust far beyond their reasoning.

The one who did just that to his daughter.

She should feel something. Guilt. Regret. Instead, she lifted her shoulders and smiled. She had tasted Fiona's soul, the way it was spiced with sins that would take most a lifetime to acquire. Most would live a lifetime and never mark their souls half as dark as Fiona's — as dark as her fathers.

There was no guilt in that. In tearing the soul from a body that had no right spreading that much darkness. Though, Poe wasn't noble. There was no righteous intent behind her actions.

She needed to feed, and she did it in a way that felt a little better.

"I don't get on my knees before anyone unless I want it. And you... you're definitely not someone to get on my knees for." She crossed the room and sat on the edge of his desk. Her hand shoved the clutter there, ignoring the shattered glass as his belongings hit the floor at her feet. "So I guess you're out of luck."

Rinaldi's eyes burned into her, his anger thick in the air. "What happens now?" he said finally. "Is this the part where the pair of you try to warn me away from my goal? Tell me all the things you'll do to me if I don't walk away and leave her be? It won't work. Do you have any idea who I am? What I've been through? The hands I've shaken? The lives I've stolen?"

Poe scoffed.

"That's supposed to mean something to us?" Dex asked.

"It means you two little shits can't scare me. I won't stop. We won't stop until she's dead."

She clicked her tongue. "Well, that won't do."

"Do you have any idea who I am?" his voice rose as he glared at her.

Her brows dropped over her eyes. "He keeps asking that. Does he honestly not know?"

Dex reached over and pressed his knuckle lightly to her cheek. "No, obnoxious people do that when they think the world is owed to them. Like who they are somehow excuses them from consequence."

"Ah." Poe lifted her shoulders. "Today is not going to be your day then. Since we're the consequences to you hunting me. And... it's not looking good."

"So what then?" Rinaldi laughed. "What now?"

"Now?" Dex moved to stand between her legs. He leaned into her, his free hand planted on the desk. He ran his nose along her neck, inhaled her before he looked at Rinaldi with milky eyes. His hand grasped her jaw, tilted her head back to look at the man who would quickly satisfy them both. Hips rolled into her as the heady scent of pleasure filled the surrounding space. Poe reached out, grabbed Rinaldi by the tie and pulled him toward them.

His pupils were blown, his mouth agape as he leaned into Poe. The threat gone from his face, the hate melted from his eyes. In its place was a pleasure that blinded him from his task. That erased his mind of the steps he took to stand before them. A blissful haze he didn't deserve but would make him taste all the more sweet.

Poe's mouth opened, her fangs glinted in the light.

"Now, we feed."

21

WOE AND JOY CAN feel so similar. They inflate your chest. Steal your breath. Make you ache with how full you feel. As he stood in the dark, a shadow at home in the night's grasp. He stood there, staring at the silhouette of frames he knew were full of photos of him, the air slightly chilled and filled with the sound of Poe's breath.

Sweet.

Steady.

Satisfied.

It was the sound of everything. Knowing that as he stood across the room and just watched her filled him to bursting. Her blood was still on his hands. It belonged there just as much as she belonged in any room he entered. Dex lifted his hand and dragged his tongue along his palm.

The taste of her was like a punch to the gut. It almost doubled him over.

Dex crossed the room, the cool night air unnoticed on his bare skin. The air would never be as cold as his flesh. Her dark curtains billowed in the slight breeze from the window. It brushed against him as he walked by, the light touch not registering to his senses. Nothing registered to him anymore. Nothing but the heat of her hands, her hot pussy, her lips.

Poe groaned. Her hand went up to shove at the bonnet on her head, making it slip and fall further down her brow.

It made him grin as he stood there, looking down at her. The top of her was bare, the sheets pooled between her legs. His eyes traced her every line, committed them to memory. From her bonnet covered brow down to the tips of her toes with their nails painted black. They wiggled as she shifted slightly.

He bent, his bloodied hands hovered over her throat.

Every night he found himself here. As though he was still the Dex from his past, the one who was too afraid to know her. Too afraid of what it would mean to keep her. He could spend an eternity watching her like this. Asleep. As vulnerable as he would ever see her.

His fingers curled. The heat of her neck so close, he could almost feel her pulse against his palms. He could see the image of them closing around her throat. The little gasp she'd make when he squeezed. The moan that would follow when her eyes rolled back, and he held on so tight, the only breath she could take would be one he allowed.

Dex's eyes closed, a groan trapped in his throat. He held it in, remembering the way he often had to swallow it down. Careful not to wake her.

This wasn't then.

His eyes snapped open, and he looked at the lightened skin, the teeth marks on the side of her throat that had all but healed. He'd marked her. A thrill moved through him as he remembered the taste of her, better than any flesh that had ever passed his lips.

The tip of his fingers lightly traced the mark. His thumb slid to the front of her throat as the rest of his fingers slid back.

Poe moaned. "Either tighten that hold and make this a good time or come back to bed." Her voice was raw, thick with sleep.

Dex's eyes snapped to her face. She looked deep in sleep still, her eyes closed, breathing steady. A grin lifted his lips as he tightened his hold.

"Tighter," she moaned.

Who was he to do anything but oblige?

"Dex." She kicked the sheets free from her legs, her arms reaching for him.

"Tighter, beautiful monster?" He climbed onto the bed, straddling her as he stared down into her dark eyes. "Beg for all your twisted delights."

"The only twisted thing I want is you."

He dipped his head and captured her lips in his. His teeth pierced the flesh around her lips, the sweet taste making him moan. Delicious and filling. His tongue dove into her mouth, blending the taste of her saliva with the blood in his own. He broke the kiss, his tongue tracing the small wound before he pressed another light one to her nose.

The idea of soulmates was something he always scoffed at. A ridiculous kind of magic that would never have a use to him. His soul couldn't be promised to someone when it didn't belong to him. Yet, it didn't belong to the witch who cursed him either. Not anymore. The longing he felt deep in his bones told him it belonged to Poe. His need to be bitten by her, devoured by her, delivered by her cursed him to exist for nothing else.

That witch would be upset if she ever found out how effort-lessly Poe wrestled his soul free from her grasp only to tie it to her own. To erase the tortured endlessness and replace it with a constant pleasure that would forever run through him.

To claim him.

"And you have me, Poe. You always will."

The End?

Afterword

I never quite know where to start with these things.

Dark and spooky stories have always been a passion of mine. When I first began writing stories, I always wrote spooky little shorts that never really amounted to anything, so the idea of releasing a monster story around Halloween has been on a goal list of mine since I published my first book in June of 2021, and I can't tell you how happy it makes me to accomplish that goal.

Poe has been a character who has been whispering in my ear for a while now, I just didn't know what story she wanted to tell. A few weeks ago, Dex came to me. What a dark and beautiful pair they made. I just knew the two of them were meant to meet. They both had an obsessive personality that made them the stuff of nightmares... which to them is practically a wet dream. I know this story may have felt a little short, but I wouldn't write this off as the end of them. They're both really loud. I have a feeling they'll be whispering another story in my ear really soon. Hopefully, enough readers like them enough to see them again.

Thanks for reading!

Acknowledgments

Being an independent author is definitely not an independent process. I have been lucky enough to find readers who have showed interest in the passion I have in writing, and thank goodness for that, or I wouldn't have the beta and ARC readers I've found along the way. I want to thank all of them for giving my story a chance and helping me make it the best story it could be (under such a tight time-frame; I know. I'm sorry... sort of). I also want to thank all the readers I've met along the way through either Instagram or BookTok. Never in my wildest dreams would I have thought there would be people out there so interested in words I've written. You'll never know how much it means to me when one of you sneaks into my DMs to rant about a story you're reading. I love, love, *love* those messages, and a lot of the time they're fuel I desperately need when I'm running low or burnt out. Thank you.

To my husband, who pauses his video games and silences his mic to listen to me go on about a story that is nothing more than an idea in my head. You're the best sounding board, and I hope you know how much I appreciate you sitting there and listening to everything I have to say. My endless rambling that has that blank stare in your eyes as you try to put together a story that I only gave you a handful of pieces for. I love you, and thank you!

To all my friends and family who constantly encourage me to keep pursuing this dream of mine, one that I didn't have the courage to even pursue until I was in my thirties, you will never know how much it means to me to come to your houses and see my books on your shelf. I will always appreciate your love and support.

Of course, to J.L. Casten. Girl, I am so sorry! I just keep throwing books at you, and you, being the amazing gift you've been since I've met you, have taken the time to read each and every one, give me your honest feedback, and help me tear it to shreds so I can build it back up to the book that finally makes it to my reader's hands. You will never know how happy I am that you messaged me that day, and I will never let go of this friendship. You're stuck with me now. (Muahahahahaha!) You're family now, and I love you to pieces. Now, if only I could get you guys to move up here to Canada, I'd be set. <3

I also want to give a huge shout out to someone who has become really special to me very quickly, LaTosha Webber! You came into my life as an excited reader who pumped me up so big, I am surprised I could get anything done. You're such a special person, with a huge heart and I am heartbroken every day we don't live closer. You give up so much of your time to talk books with me, to listen to me rant about disrespectful characters and my life, even when I know you have your plate full. You're an amazing person, and I hope for the best and brightest things for you in your life. You deserve it.

A big thanks to anyone in the booktok community who has helped me grow! You guys make or break authors, and I am forever thankful to get all the support and recs you throw my way.

SJ

About Author

S.J. Stewart is a Canadian author who lives in the bustling city of Toronto with her husband and toddler. She wrote her first novel when she was sixteen and never stopped writing, though she didn't get around to publishing her first work until 2021.

She is a genre jumper and dabbles in everything, but her published work is Paranormal Fantasy and Romance. Her goal is to get all the stories out of her head before they slowly drive her to madness.

Be sure to find her on social media for updates, new releases, and exclusive content.

https://sjstewartbooks.ca/

https://twitter.com/shayystewartt

https://www.facebook.com/authorsjstewart

https://www.tiktok.com/@shaygirlshaaay

Also By

**Someone is hunting them in a realm she's
sure she doesn't belong.**

Melas wakes in the Dark Realm with all her
memories suddenly missing. She knows there
are black spaces in her mind, darkness keeping who and what she is hidden from her,
if only she knew why. All she has is her in-
stincts, and they're screaming at her:

Protect. Fight. Survive.

Scars riddling her body tell her she'd been running for a long
time. Though who's hunting them is a mystery, Melas knows
she will stop at nothing to protect her five-year-old daughter,
Zura. Landed in the laps of three men determined to solve the
mystery of who they are, Melas is unable to let her guard down
enough to let Ridhor, Andrei, or Orren in.

Berserker. Incubus. Vampire.

There are some things you just can't forget, the warrior she is has been carved into her soul, etched on her bones. That warrior will fight with everything she is to protect the ones she loves. She doesn't know how she came to run, but if they ever catch up to her, she will set their world on fire.

Read the first in the Seven Realms books and start your journey into the realms with Melas, Zura, Ridhor, Andrei, and Orren. Available on Amazon.

Lennox lived the kind of life that never allowed her to relinquish control. She felt responsible for her sister, for her mother, for their finances, for managing the family struggles and protecting all the people she held dear. Her life was a weight on her shoulders she could never escape. When her protectiveness lands her before a judge, causing her to lose her job, she realizes she might just have to do something she never thought she would.

Jaxon Smith never thought he would see Lennox again. He also never thought when he did, she wouldn't remember him. She looked through him, as though they didn't share that special night all those years ago, like he meant nothing. Realizing her life was slowly becoming a sinking ship, Jax did the one thing he knew how, spread his money around and made her an offer she couldn't refuse.

He doesn't really need a girlfriend, but paying her to be his was the only thing he could think of to keep her around long enough to get her to see that surrendering all her control to him is exactly what she needs.

This billionaire romance is available on Amazon.

Newsletter Story Preview

P LEASE ENJOY THE FIRST few chapters to a story exclusive to my newsletter. If you enjoy what you read, feel free to hop onto my website to subscribe and get the episodes for free!

SJ STEWART

Inside
the
Shadow
that
Bleeds

Content Warning

H EY READER,

This is a dark story that is filled with things that may not sit right with every reader. There will be scenes of mental and physical torture. There will be scenes of violence that will include some blood and gore. There will be scenes that are explicitly sexual in nature. There will be times where the main character questions her grasp on reality that may be triggering to some readers.

Though I've done my best to identify things in this story that may not sit right with some readers and give them a clear idea of what they are in store for, triggers are very personal. It is not my intention to willfully omit something that could be upsetting to my readers.

Please be advised before you go any further.

Chapter One

SHADOW

"Have you ever looked into the shadows and thought they were home? That the dark corners in your room were actually doors opened wide, and you'd find the only embrace you'd ever need if only you were brave enough to step through?" Her short fingernails, chipped as the black polish surrendered its hold from the tips, picked at a thread along the seam of the armchair. It was cozy, a comfortable canvas in a pleasant enough beige. Her feet rested sloppily on the floor. The toes of her worn sneakers dug into the area rug in a similar grey, her ankles loose. Her eyes looked at the many shades of grey in a room where she spent so much time. Anything to avoid the eyes of the woman who was much her diary. A confessional she poured all her thoughts into.

"I can't say I have." Her pen moved along the pad in her lap, though her eyes were on Shadow. They always were. An intense gaze that burned and ached. Delved just a bit too deep, a blade aimed to slice through her flesh. "Why do you think you feel that way?"

A question for a question.

Never answers. Not really. That's not what she was there for. She was a guide, meant to shine light toward where she wanted Shadow to go.

It was fucking annoying.

"Because the shadows seemed to be the only thing that ever wanted me," she answered. It was an answer she gave often. Partly because it was the one that felt right, but also because she enjoyed the way it made that muscle twitch in Dr. Reed's jaw when she said it. Knew how much she disliked the answer, much like Shadow disliked her answering all her questions with a question.

"I can see why you feel that way, but you know that's not true." She wrote away on her pad. Her pen was ceaseless.

"Do I?" Shadow raised a brow.

"Miss Graves." Her tone was the patronizing one a mother would use when her child was being difficult. At thirty-four, she was far from being a child.

Shadow Graves.

Such an ominous name given to a haunted little girl who stepped out of the shadows of the night. It was almost funny when she thought about the way a dark cloud hung overhead, the way her nights were endless whispers that called to her, begged her toward something. Somewhere.

The man in the corner.

"Let's talk about that night," Dr. Reed tried to redirect her thoughts.

Shadow sighed. It was always about that night. The single night where she began, all the nights before as blank and dark as the endless pitch she sometimes felt she was bound to.

"Let's go back."

"Haven't we gone back enough?" Shadow's brow rose, and for the first time since she sat down, she looked at the woman in the room. She was in her late forties, with taut, deep brown skin. Dr. Reed parted her hair in the centre, pulled back into a neat bun at her nape. She should look stern, but her brown eyes were soft, which made her look kind. Made people want to surrender their secrets to her. Her pencil skirt was black, her white shirt crisp and tucked in at her waist. She wore sensible shoes. Black with a low chunky heel. Her ankles crossed.

Even as she stared at Shadow, willed her to participate in the session, there was a softness to her gaze. As intense as it felt. "If we had, we would have the answers you want."

Another sigh left her, but she rested her head back on the chair and closed her eyes. She hated going back as much as she loved it. Felt the way the memory covered her flesh and burrowed into her bone and made that place in her mind where nothing lived anymore pulse.

So she went back.

"The air is hot, but the cement is so cold on my feet. Each step feels a little like stepping on glass. A sharpness that bites into the soles." The night played behind her eyes. "My brow was feverish. I felt the stream of blood drip from my temple down to my chin. It dripped on the top of my feet every few steps. It kept time. The constant *drip, drip, drip*." Her voice fell away. She could feel her lips move, but she was so far away from that room and Dr. Reed.

Twenty-seven years in the past.

It was so dark. It shouldn't be that dark with the street lights evenly spaced and lining the small neighbourhood, but it was like the night held hands over the light. Stifled them. Every step felt like it went in the wrong direction. Something at her back screamed at her to turn around, but she didn't, and she couldn't remember why.

She couldn't remember anything.

Her throat was so tight. It strangled her, stole away the sobs she desperately wanted to set free. A howl sounded. It was everywhere and nowhere. Pressed against her ear, breathed against her skin. The louder it sounded, the darker it got. A gust of wind blew away all the light. Deep and sticky.

'Stop it,' she whimpered. Her voice was so small. Her hands reached up and clamped over her ears. 'Stop it.'

The darkness was loud. It pushed into her ears and filled her head up with shadows.

'Stop it!'

The night wrapped a hand around her and squeezed. Each breath struggled to fill a chest with no space in it as pressure made her want to double over. Fall to her knees.

Her teeth chattered and her eyes fogged over.

She was going to die.

Not from the blood that left a steady stream down her face, not from the cold that bit down into the bones of her feet, but from the vast nothingness that tried to squeeze her into nothing too.

As fast as it came, it was gone.

She blinked hard. Clamped her eyes closed. The tears left their place on her lids to stream down her face. Opening her eyes, she looked up.

There he was.

A man.

Clad in black, his wide-brimmed hat cast his face in complete shadow. He stood there in the middle of the street. His legs shoulder length apart as he stared at her, his eyes white beams that glowed in the dark.

She was scared. He was so much bigger than her.

Black shadows reached out from the darkness. Phantom hands that wrapped around him, and made him disappear from his place.

She whimpered.

The shadows pulled away, and in the man's place was a boy. He was the same size as her, maybe just a hair taller. Half his face was cast in shadow, but the other half was a deep brown. He smiled, his eyes bright as he stared at her and held out a hand.

Hesitation rooted her feet in place. She couldn't trust him. He'd come from the same shadows that screamed at her. The ones that raked wretched fingers down her back and promised pain if she didn't listen.

His hand was steady. Darkness ate away at the edges of his nails, but his hand looked warm. Everything inside her wanted to take it.

She shook her head. Her bottom lip quivered and her chin wrinkled. Fresh tears pushed their way out of her eyes and left a slow trail down her cheeks. She couldn't trust him. She just couldn't. She couldn't trust anybody.

His eyes slowly rose and looked up at the sky.

Helpless to do anything else, her gaze followed his. The shadows danced in the low light overhead. Wisps of obsidian like smoke exhaled from something dark and malicious. It was like they stood inside something. A snow globe that kept them safe inside while something profane tried to get in, but couldn't.

Because of him.

It was a captivating sight, one that held all her attention until she felt the burn of his gaze on her face. Dropping her head, she looked at him. At his outstretched hand.

And she took it.

They walked together in the dark. The strength of his hand fought off the fear she wore like her skin. They walked through the night until the sun took its first bite out of the sky. Until it lightened, and those wisps disappeared from overhead.

His eyes kept their brightness when he looked at her. Stars set in a sheet of black in their vibrancy. They stood there for what felt like forever. Until the last bits of night left the sky and they stood in the sun's warmth.

She wanted to hold on to him forever, but the hand in hers disappeared.

"Where did he go?" Dr. Reed asked.

Shadow swallowed hard. A sniffle sounded, her throat suddenly raw. "I looked around, and I was standing alone. At least... I thought I was."

"Weren't you?" she asked.

No. She looked down and there was a dog at her side. Small, black, with eyes that glowed like stars in the darkest sky. "I guess I was," she lied. "That's how they found me."

"Who was the boy?" Dr. Reed asked.

Opening her eyes, she pursed her lips as she slowly lifted her head from the back of the chair. "I don't know."

"Do you believe there was a boy there with you, Shadow? Before the police found you?"

Yes. "No. The man he was before... he's the same one I see every night."

Dr. Reed nodded slowly. "The figment attached to your sleep paralysis."

"My sleep demon." Shadow chuckled. "Seems fitting, right? Since he's the demon that haunts me the most."

"Why do you think he's the person you see?" Dr. Reed inquired.

She thought about it and shrugged it off. Some things were better to keep to herself. "He was a man, then a boy... then a dream. Seems fitting he should haunt my nights."

The timer went off, and they both looked up. "That's all the time we have for today, Shadow. I would love for you to think about your *sleep demon* and try to figure out why he's the man you thought you saw all those years ago."

"Does it matter?" Did it really matter who held the frail ribbon of her sanity in their hand and gave it the gentle tug it took to unravel her? Shouldn't it only matter that she was being unravelled?

"Memories like this are like a door. We have to figure out how to open them to see what's hiding on the other side." She closed the leather over her pad and set it on the table next to her chair before she got to her feet. "I think who you were before you became Shadow Graves might be on the other side of this memory."

Standing, Shadow nodded. "See you in a few weeks." She walked to the door, pausing with her hand on the doorknob. "Dr. Reed?"

"Yes, Shadow."

"This memory... this door... what happens if I don't like what's behind it?" *Blood dripped down her face, keeping time. Drip, drip, drip.*

The smile on her face was warm. "Sometimes we have to turn over stones to look at what's underneath. More often than not, we don't like it... but we can't heal from wounds we can't find."

Nodding, Shadow smiled solemnly over her shoulder. "Right."

The trouble was, these days, she felt like she was nothing more than open wounds that would never heal.

"Shadow."

"Hmm."

"This demon of yours, the boy from your past, name them. Get to know them. Make them real. Maybe then you can use them to help you find your way."

The boy from her past had a name. He whispered it to her as they walked through the night, hand in hand.

Raef.

Chapter Two

SHADOW

THERE WAS ALWAYS SOMETHING so cleansing about stepping out onto the street after a session. She often paused with her hand on the glass door and just stared out. In a way, it was like this door was like that snow globe all those years ago. Her safe inside while the world thrummed on just outside the glass.

Shadow stepped onto the sidewalk. She reached into her crossbody bag, pulled out her shades and put them on. Shadow turned her face up and let the warmth of the sun kiss her face. It felt too hot, stirred her skin in a way that itched. It felt too bright, like it would erase all the parts of her shroud in shadow and nothing would be left. Just a pile of clothes on the sidewalk where she used to be.

Shadow wrapped her hands around herself as she walked down Parliament Street toward her apartment.

It was a busy street for what it was. Old buildings with modern storefronts. Coffee shops, pizza joints, convenience stores and the likes. Her lips vibrated together, and she blew a rogue curl back from her face. With hands dug in her pockets, she walked down a street she knew well. She used to walk up this street from her elementary school as a kid, hang out in the pet store and dreamt of a time when she could have a pet. Company that would always be hers, no matter what anyone thought of her or said.

No matter how loud the shadows whispered or shouted.

The foot traffic wasn't as heavy as downtown. There weren't any sights to see on Parliament Street, just people who called this neighbourhood theirs. Shadow kept her head down, avoiding the friendly smiles as treacherous as bared teeth. They were a mask, something sweet not meant for her.

Her mind went over the session with her therapist as she looked over her shoulder. The hairs on the back of her neck stood on end. Her skin pebbled, despite the warmth that should be in the air, even in September.

If the memory she had of that night was some door — locked and secured, preventing her from seeing back into her past — could Dr. Reed be right? Was Raef somehow the key?

He was as much hers now as he was that night all those nights ago. He stood in the darkness of her room like smoke that blew in on the breeze. The scent of him filled up every space, a chilled dampness of an evening spent in the woods with nothing but the light of moon to light her way. He froze her there in her bed, her eyes glued to him as the darkness seeped into the walls from the corner like the room steeped in it.

Then out he'd step.

Tall, dark... terrifying. Or at least he would be, if he hadn't been with her for so long. If he hadn't made the shadows something she looked forward to seeing, longed for. Because she knew he would arrive when they did, and he'd keep the parts that reeked with a stench of something profane and malevolent at bay.

She tensed, her feet stumbling as something dragged down her back.

Something not really there, with a breath that blew her hair over her shoulder.

Her step quickened.

The shadows stalked her even in the light of day. It was endless torture that somehow got better at night. Confidence she didn't feel during the day leached into her skin. A breathy voice that whispered the night was hers.

If only she could feel the smallest fraction of that during the day.

Her paranoia stemmed from existing in a world she felt constantly meant out to harm her since she'd been unable to figure out who shattered her all those years ago. Or at least, that was what Dr. Reed told her. That was why diving into her past seemed so important.

Life had shown that was very much the case.

Regardless of what happened to her at the tender age of seven, that was just the first hit in her constant bout with life and the universe that kept it. Foster homes, cruel guardians, bullies, faceless men in the night. The life she lived made her wary of everyone.

Her therapist may think that was paranoid, but Shadow knew it would be stupid to live any other way. How many people would shove their hand through the bars of a cage after being bit by the animal inside? Who in their right mind wouldn't fear the sting of teeth in their skin?

She wasn't paranoid.

Life proved her right every single time.

Her feet paused as she passed the second coffee shop. She could really use some caffeine to take the edge off, to soothe the frayed parts of her that fired circuits of reluctance and anxiety through her. She groaned low, regretting not stopping at the one further up the street. This one always got her order wrong and then tried to convince her just how wrong she'd been in explaining what she wanted.

'It's because you said 'French vanilla iced coffee' and there is no iced coffee in French vanilla. Only vanilla. You got a French vanilla coffee.'

Shadow groaned low.

Made sense. Why clarify when you could spend five minutes trying to convince a customer to take an order they didn't want? Just chuck out the whole *iced* part and hand her a steaming hot coffee... because that's definitely what she meant.

Digging into her bag, she grabbed a fistful of change and dropped it in the worn cup of the man who held the door for her. He had a gaping smile that wrinkled his eyes and was a bit hunched over. He wasn't the man she usually saw out there, and for a moment, she wondered just where he went.

Did he disappear? Just another homeless man no one could account for because they didn't know he was there in the first place?

She frowned.

As she stood in line, her eyes looking up at the menu even though she knew what she wanted and wasn't looking at any of the items listed there, she hoped he didn't disappear. Hoped there was someone out there who knew where he was. Who knew *who* he was.

Why did that bother her so much?

Because no one knew who she was either.

At the front of the line, she made her very specific and slowly spoken order and was pleasantly surprised when she got just what she asked for.

Your day is looking up, Shadow.

At the door, she handed the man one of the sandwiches she ordered, a donut and a bottle of water and continued to her small apartment on The Esplanade. A small part of her worried her little neighbourhood was fast moving toward a *rejuvenation project*. All that meant was overpriced tiny condos and townhouses that pushed the low-income families out of the city. Big parks, city buildings that boasted being there for a community they'd chased away with the big price tags. Regent Park had been the first to go, but the project burned out quickly and Shadow secretly wished they couldn't find the funds to finish it.

All those glass high-rises and their sleek designs were an eyesore. Every time she blinked, another one went up.

Corporate fuckers.

Shadow cupped her iced-coffee in the crook of her arm held at her side as she devoured her sandwich. Nothing like deep diving into the cockles of her mind to work up an appetite. Once done, she crumpled the wrapper and held it in her closed fist as she gulped her coffee like water. She'd wait until the next lights and toss it in the trash.

It was a pretty uneventful walk. It usually was.

Still, her shoulders were tense. The hairs on the back of her neck on end.

Someone is behind you.

The voice in her head screamed at her, but like so many other voices in her life, she ignored it.

By the time she got onto The Esplanade, her patience had completely worn thin. If there was someone following her, they were going to learn the hard way that Shadow Graves wasn't the one. Hand in her bag, she wrapped her fist around the metal pen she kept in there.

Footsteps. Not the normal, every day crowd, but ones that matched pace with hers. Heavy.

She whirled, pen raised.

Her eyes widened when she looked back at nothing.

"Great," she huffed. "You're losing your mind." She chuckled again as she shoved the pen back in her bag. "Can't really lose something you never had though, right?"

An old man looked at her as he walked by, brows raised, before he scurried past.

"And now you're talking to yourself. Great. Just great."

Her eyes dropped, and she froze.

There, at her feet on the sidewalk, was a dog. His fur was the sheen of shadows moving through the night. An endless obsidian kissed with the silver of smoke and moonlight. His ears were tall and menacing. Pointed up and almost the length of his entire head. He rivalled her in size. Was likely bigger than she was. Heavier, she was certain of that. Muscles and sinew was a tapestry under taut skin covered in the dark, short hair.

His eyes shone in a familiar way that made her heart hammer in her chest. Their eyes locked, and she froze. A part of her wanted to bend, to squat low and get a better look at him, but all she could do was stand where she was, and stare.

What the hell kind of dog was this?

He looked more pony than dog and like he was something more at home guarding Hades' gates.

Throat suddenly as dry as desert, she lifted her iced coffee and sipped. The sound of liquid trying to be sucked past the ice into her straw sounded as loud as a gunshot in her ears as the dog cocked his head to the side.

Swallowing hard, she lowered her cup. "Are you real?"

There was no telling anymore. She spent every night staring at a man she was almost positive wasn't, the same man who was somehow man and boy and dog all those years ago, so she really wasn't the best judge of the corporeal world.

...and dog.

Her brow quirked up. "Is it you?" she whispered.

A breath huffed out of him before he turned tail and took off down the street.

Shadow watched him go, unsure of whether she watched anything at all.

"Shadow Graves, the mysterious woman with a few screws loose," she murmured to herself before she turned and slammed into something.

All the air left her lungs as her feet went up, and her ass hit pavement. A chill moved down her spine, jagged and unforgiving. It was a frigid burn that made beads of sweat cover her brow. Her eyes searched the surrounding space, but she was just as alone as she'd ever been.

Ass on the pavement and a look of bewilderment on her face, there was nothing to slam into. No one there who could have knocked her off her feet.

"What the fuck?" she groaned.

Her chest ached. It felt like she ran full speed into a brick wall —not that she'd ever done that. If she had, this was exactly how she imagined she'd feel. Sore and a little embarrassed.

A finger pressed to her chest where her heart raced, and pain sat on her skin. Her eyes narrowed at the air above her and she sucked in a shaky breath.

Black wisps moved through the air, so faint, she almost couldn't see them at all. No more noticeable than cigarette smoke that plumed up into the sky. Shadow's brow dropped as she shook her head, something tight lodged in her throat.

This wasn't real. It couldn't be. None of this was real.

A growl sounded at her back.

Her head whipped behind her, and the mysterious dog stood there. His head dropped between his shoulders, his lips curled up to reveal teeth that looked too long and extremely sharp. Thick ropes of saliva fell from his lips.

What the fuck was happening?

Her heart lurched up in her throat as she thought about being caught between some weird shadow and the hellbeast at her back. She didn't think she would be enough to stop either.

If this was real.

It wasn't.

Couldn't be, right?

If she believed in a higher power, now would be the time to ask for a little help. Or maybe ask them to take these two things back wherever they belonged. Hell. The Underworld. The Abyss. She didn't really know. What she did know was these were the kinds of things that existed in the dark corners of her mind, not in the streets of Toronto.

Her head whipped forward, and she stared at clear air.

Brow dropped, she turned and looked at the empty sidewalk behind her.

No shadows. No dogs.

What. The. Fuck.

She sat there on the ground, debating walking back up to her therapist. Clearly, they had a lot more to work through. Eventually, she got tired of the people casting weird looks at her as they walked around her on the sidewalk and she forced herself to her feet.

Home. That was the first step.

Back to her small bachelor's apartment and the walls she knew. What came after wouldn't be up to her. It never was. At least in the comfort of home, her demons could torment her without an audience.

Chapter Three

SHADOW

A MIND IS APPARENTLY a terrible thing to lose, but hers never belonged to her. It toyed with her, tormented her, haunted her, but it wasn't hers. Not really. It belonged to the very shadows they named her after. The ones that slunk through every inch of a mind never meant to be anything but dark.

It was all very dramatic.

Leaned back against the door of her apartment, she tossed her keys into the metal bowl on the table beside it and blew a strand of hair back from her face.

What a day.

It began with an alarm clock that refused to go off when it was supposed to, a hurry out of her apartment, a run up the street to her therapist's office where they reached hands into her mind and tried to tear it open and look inside. As though that wasn't enough, she was being stalked by an imaginary dog, seeing shadows and slamming into nothing on the street.

Just fabulous.

The only thing that made the day better was knowing it wasn't even two yet.

The chuckle that left her was wild. A sound of something captive slammed against a cage that made the bars rattle. Shaking her head at the absurdity that was her life, she strut to the small kitchen to her left and tossed out her cup. She braced her hand on the counter after she pushed the cupboard where she hit her trash bin closed and just looked out at the apartment.

She'd set up her living room space right in front of the kitchen area, nothing more but bar stools pushed under the small counter in front of her as seating to eat. The counter only sat two, which was one more than she'd ever need. Her couch was small — a loveseat they called them — and black. A rectangular black coffee table sat in front of it and her TV was mounted on the wall in front of that. There was just enough space for her to walk between the coffee table and the TV. Other than that, the only other furniture in her living room were the two tall lamps in the corners — one by the window and one right beside the counter. They had silver poles and cylinder black shades.

Shadow didn't need much.

There was no one in her life to share her space with, so this was more than enough.

Behind her loveseat was her bedroom area. A Queen bed centred in the wall with black and white geometric bedding on it. She could see the front door from her bed. Sometimes she would lie there and think of what she would do if someone came bursting in.

Most of the time, she thought she'd do nothing at all. She'd just lay there and see what came next. She should probably talk to Dr. Reed about that. About her lack of reaction. The thought she didn't really care what would come next. What happened to her.

There was a small hall to the right of her front door that had two closets, one she used as a bedroom closet, and the other she used for storage, with her bathroom at the end. It was an average sized bathroom, though she couldn't know for sure. She had nothing to compare it to but the other places she'd lived. It didn't seem much smaller or bigger than any of those. Toilet, sink, tub and shower combo.

It was functional, and that was all she cared about.

The walls were the same white they were when she moved in. There were no framed pictures or decor hung. She had no desire to see anything but white. A contrast to her very being.

A hand dragged against her face, and she sighed.

Her ears rang. The sound filled all the space in her head, made it buzz. Her eyes opened, and she looked at the apartment she knew. With the window with a view of nothing — the brick of the neighbouring building — and her simple furniture.

Darkness ate at the corners, and black film covered the windowpanes. The shadows moved like a million tiny spiders that climbed over everything. They devoured the plain white walls she knew so well, accompanied by the high whine that made her feel unbalanced.

Her throat was so tight. It strangled her, stole away the sobs she desperately wanted to set free. A howl sounded. It was everywhere and nowhere. Pressed against her ear, breathed against her skin. The louder it sounded, the darker it got. A gust of wind blew away all the light. Deep and sticky.

'Stop it,' she whimpered. Her hands clamped over her ears. 'Stop it.'

The shadows didn't listen to her, they never had. Instead, they intensified with her distress.

'Stop it!'

She felt heat on her lip. Her tongue ran along it, and the bitter taste of blood filled her mouth. It thinned her saliva and churned her stomach. Her eyes rolled back in her head as her knees buckled.

"Stop it!"

Black wisps of smoke moved through the apartment. They looked like people, almost, but their limbs were too long. Like something dark pretending to be people, and that was as close as they could manage. The smoke billowed around the edges, as though keeping the form was tedious.

First just one, then another. And another. Until all that existed in her apartment was shadows, figures, and the high scream of the dark.

Shadow's head spun. The taste of bile mixed with the blood in her mouth as she slumped back against the stove behind her. There were no men here that would transform into little boys who held her hand through the treacherous night. There were no hellbeasts that looked like dogs.

It was just Shadow and pain. Pain that looked like dark figures meant to do her harm.

She fell to her knees, her hands clamped around her ears. She didn't know why she bothered. It did nothing to silence the high screech that felt like drills aimed at her brain.

She was going to die. That thought threw her back in time.

Her teeth chattered as her eyes fogged over.

She was going to die.

Not from the blood that left a steady stream down her face, not from the cold that bit down into the bones of her feet, but from the vast nothingness that tried to squeeze her into nothing too.

Her eyes searched for her salvation.

He would come. He had to come. If he didn't come, she wouldn't survive this. Her vision tunnelled as her chest filled with smoke and the smell of brimstone swirled around her.

Clad in black, his wide-brimmed hat cast his face in complete shadow. He stood there in the middle of the street. His legs shoulder length apart as he stared at her, his eyes white beams that glowed in the dark.

He would come.

Please! She internally begged for him.

A figure stepped forward. Eyes were shining rubies as it looked down at her and lifted a sinister hand. Its fingers were long and tapered like blades. The tip pressed under her chin, plunged into her flesh as it lifted her head. Pain shot through her. The tip embedded in her flesh was a circuit, and it sent waves and waves of agony through her. It was so intense, she felt it in her bones. Deeper still. She was sure she felt it down to her very soul.

The pitch smoke parted where its mouth should be, and shock filled her. Inside, fire swirled. Molten lava and burning embers.

Her hands clamped so tightly on her ears, she wondered if it spoke to her. If maybe it whispered ways to escape the torment she found herself entrenched in.

A part of her wanted to risk her sanity and remove her hands from her ears. Another part warned she would likely suffer more than a nosebleed if she did.

As the pain amped up, her body stiffened and her hands fell away from her ears. She slumped back against her fridge, the black curtains of unconsciousness closing slowly over her eyes.

The gargled whine that left the phantom figure's mouth wasn't what she expected. It was the haunted sound of too many voices to count. An ear curdling sound of a possessed crowd as they howled and screamed — desperate to be heard. It made her blood chill. The familiar heat in her ears, accompanied by a slow trail of warmth, told her it made her ears bleed. The talon felt like it ripped through the thin flesh under her jaw up into her mouth. It filled her mouth with the taste of ash as she struggled with everything in her to stay awake. To stay present.

She should let go, she realized.

There was nothing in this moment she wanted.

Sleep would be better. Hell, death would be better.

Just let go, Shadow. Let go.

The voice in her head suddenly wasn't hers. There was no snark, no attitude. There was no despondency. It was a deep growl, one that rumbled through her mind and made her eyes slip closed.

Surrender.

It would be so easy.

Fear moved like ice through her veins, chased by an all-encompassing chill of relief. Weightless and wonderful. She should have surrendered all those years ago. The admission felt hazy. Something she would think while she was drunk, and she lost some of her faculties. Back when the blood dripped from her brow and kept moving down. Counted down the moments. When the chill of the frigid street sliced into her feet like broken glass.

She should have surrendered.

Let go.

Disappeared into the endless dark.

The pain burned brightly through her until there was nothing left to burn. Until all her nerves felt so fried, they short-circuited and left nothing but numbness behind. She liked the numb. The way it was ravenous and devoured everything inside her, leaving nothing behind.

Let go, Shadow.

Okay. Yeah. She would.

She would fall into the numbness that held her tighter than anyone else ever had.

That wasn't entirely true. He held her tightly once. The grip of his hand more comfort than she ever received or ever would again. With his hand in hers, they walked through the endless night until they created an end all on their own. Carved it in the dark with their combined strength.

No.

The numb stole the thought away.

Letting go was better than remembering.

Shadow's eyes fell closed, her muscles limp.

Knock, knock, knock.

White hot pain filled her. The taste of ash left her mouth as she sucked in a breath that made her groan. Her hand whipped out. She grabbed hold of the handle of the fridge as her eyes whipped open and she looked around her bland apartment.

Normal with its white walls and bare furniture.

Not even a whisper of a shadow remained, as her body tensed and her eyes watered. Coughing, her brow dropped as thick globs of black landed on her linoleum floors. Splatters of tar. She coughed again, the taste of ash gave way to the taste of blood and bile.

"Fucking hell," Shadow groaned.

Knock, knock, knock.

Her eyes went to the door.

Knock, knock, knock.

Shadow's legs shook as she forced them under her. She kept her hold on the fridge as she pulled herself to her feet and stood. A moment passed where she tested the strength of her legs before she stumbled toward the door.

Knock, knock, knock.

"I'm coming," she rasped. Her throat felt torn up. Dried ribbons that couldn't push sound through them.

Shaky hands pulled open the door.

The man on the other side wore an orange vest and a generic uniform. Khaki pants, sensible shoes — likely steel toed — and a grey polo. He held a small box under his arm, a tablet in the other. Thick black hair swept back from his brow and he smelled of strong cologne.

"Shadow Graves," he read slowly. His brow cocked, and a smile moved over his face. Brown cheeks covered in thick black stubble looked way too round when he smiled. Suddenly, he was a cherub instead of a man.

Cute, her tired mind thought.

"That can't be your real name."

"Unfortunately," her gravelly voice answered.

His dark brown eyes moved over her, took her in. She knew she likely looked like hot shit baked on a summer sidewalk — that's definitely how she felt. "Well, then... *Miss Graves*... this is for you then. Can you sign here?"

Shadow Graves didn't have a friend in the world. Who the hell would send her anything?

Her brow dropped, suspicion slicing through her to introduce itself to the pain that still seared her nerves. "From who?"

There was a slight pause where he just stared at her before he grabbed the box and turned it to read the label. "Says here, Dade Bruns." He read and re-read the name before he shook his head. Likely chalking all this up to some kind of joke.

She didn't find it funny. "I don't know any *Dade Bruns.*"

A forced smile shifted his lips. "Look. I just deliver the packages. I don't know who sends them, I don't know why they're sent. I just drive the truck and hand them off." He held out his tablet. "Can you sign here, please?"

It wasn't this guy's fault she was having a shit day. A huff of breath left her as she grabbed the stylus he offered and signed for the package. She took it when he held it out, noted it wasn't overly large, nor was it heavy, before she gave him a quick nod. "Awesome, thanks," she murmured low before she closed the door.

The cool steel of the door hit her back as she slumped against it, her legs still weak under her. She temporarily forgot the box in her hands as her eyes scanned the apartment for some sign of the hell she just went through.

Everything looked so *normal.*

Nothing out of place.

"Sanity, I never knew you," she groaned to herself. Her hand brushed the underside of her jaw. The flesh there was tender, but intact.

Her steps to the couch were slow, her feet weighed down by more than just the events of the day. She slumped back on the couch, the box on her lap. Her eyes traced the edges, her hands rested at her sides. She couldn't summon the strength she needed to do more than just stare at it.

Who the hell would send her anything?

"Dade Bruns, apparently," Shadow answered her own question. Dade Bruns. What the hell kind of name was that?

What kind of name was Shadow Graves? She really shouldn't judge.

Time ticked on.

She didn't know how long she sat there, but the sky darkened slightly outside before she lifted her hands and tore at the tape. With the flaps peeled back, she looked into the box.

Only three items sat inside.

Shadow frowned as she pulled out the first sheet of worn paper. She unfolded it, and confusion surged through her.

It was a map. An old one. Weathered on thick paper. If she didn't know any better, she would think it was a treasure map a pirate would carry around, but she was no pirate and she didn't have a life that would reward her with treasure. Her life was more the *continuous torment of tortured souls painted with heavy slashes of sin* type of thing. Though, she couldn't remember sinning so badly as to warrant the company she had earlier.

Unsure of what to do with it, she set it on the coffee table before she pulled out the other two items in the box.

A letter with her name scribbled on the front of the envelope sealed with one of those old red wax stamps she wasn't sure if she'd ever seen in person was the first thing she inspected. There was a shotgun, and a whip crossed through the circle seal, with a name scribbled there she couldn't quite make out.

Lips pursed in thought, she shrugged as she tossed it on the table alongside the weird map.

The last thing in the box brought no clarity.

It was heavier than she thought it would be as she held it between her finger and thumb, inspecting it. It was iron. Old. With a symbol that matched the seal on her letter.

A key.